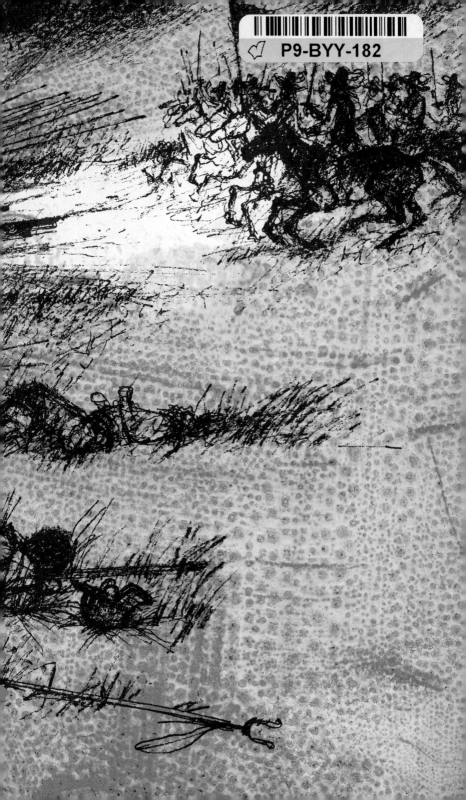

Witch Dog

By John and Patricia Beatty

At the Seven Stars
Campion Towers
The Royal Dirk

By Patricia Beatty

Bonanza Girl
Indian Canoe-maker
The Nickel-Plated Beauty
The Queen's Own Grove
Squaw Dog

Marston Moor ✕

● York
Hull

● Liverpool

Nottingham ● Newark

Shrewsbury ● Lichfield
● Leicester
● Birmingham
● Coventry
Worcester ● *Edgehill* ✕ ● Warwick ● Cambridge
Powick Bridge ✕
Gloucester ● Oxford ✕ *Chalgrove Field*
Abingdon ● *Turnham Green*
✕ *Bristol* Reading ●
London
✕ *Newbury* Dover ●

👑 The King's Headquarters

🚩 Prince Rupert's Headquarters

✕ Battles

WITCH DOG

John and Patricia Beatty

William Morrow and Company New York

To Stephanie

Contents

Foreword

Horses have often been associated with outstanding military leaders as their particular animal favorites—dogs rarely. We know, however, that Prince Rupert who was the son of the king and queen of Bohemia, German rulers, and nephew of King Charles I of England greatly favored no horse but a dog named Boye. Boye, a huge poodle, became an almost legendary figure of that terrible mid-seventeenth-century conflict, the English Civil War, a war in which Prince Rupert took part as a cavalry commander for King Charles.

Boye was born in Austria some time around 1637, but it was as an "English" dog that he won his fame. An object of hatred and terror to his master's foes, he frequently was called a "witch dog."

Many facts are known of this renowned soldier's dog. He is mentioned in memoirs of men who lived then and is the subject of pamphlet cartoons sketched by the Roundheads, the forces of Parliament, who were King Charles's, Rupert's, and Boye's enemies in battle. Although this novel is fiction, we have attempted to use existing factual material about Boye as much as possible.

Chapter I

The Earl's Gift

SIX LONG WEEKS after his master, Thomas Howard, the Earl of Arundel, had sent him forth, the messenger from England finally reached Vienna on a wet spring night of 1638. Herr Aretz, the earl's agent in Vienna, received the young man in his small private closet. After he had greeted the tall, booted, and spurred Englishman in the travel-stained cloak and given him a cup of wine, the Viennese took the letter that the courier had carried halfway across Europe.

Aretz put his fingernail beneath the seal of the now begrimed but still folded paper and broke it. While he unfolded it, he said, "What am I to find for your master this time? Does he desire another piece of sculpture, perhaps? Or does he wish me to buy a particular painting for him?"

As Herr Aretz read the letter, his yellowish eyebrows

rose slightly in surprise at what he found in it. "*Himmel!*" he exclaimed. "This time Arundel desires something alive! I am to purchase a dog—a large white dog—to be a gift from him to Prince Rupert, the prisoner in the castle at Linz."

The messenger's face lighted up at the sound of the Prince's name. Rupert was his idol, his exact age—but at nineteen years already a famous soldier. A son of the Queen of Bohemia, who was the sister of England's King Charles, Rupert's name was on the lips of many Englishmen. The young courier knew that the King's nephew, while fighting for the Bohemian cause, had been taken prisoner of war by the Austrians.

"Prince Rupert!" The messenger's voice was awestruck. "I never had a chance to see him when he was in England."

"An impressive sight, they say. Very tall and very fierce, with hair as black as sea coals. Rupert the Devil. His own brothers and sisters call him that, I've heard." Aretz laughed shortly. "And I'm to find him a dog!"

Aretz raised his voice and called out, "Johann!" Instantly the servant, an old man in a red coat and blue breeches, entered for he had been standing throughout the conversation just outside the door. "Johann, I am to buy a dog, a large white one, for one of my patrons, the Earl of Arundel. Do you know where I can find such an animal?"

Johann bowed. He did not seem surprised at all. His opinion of Englishmen was not high. They were mad, quite mad. "*Ja,* master, *ja.* Baron von Furstenberg. He has dogs—

the finest in all Vienna. They are *pudelhunde*. Huge dogs—hunters. Perhaps he would sell one."

The tiny white puppy lay fast asleep curled up within himself inside a basket. A fierce jolt shook the coach that Herr Aretz's four horses were pulling swiftly westward from Vienna. The little poodle opened his eyes sleepily and looked, blinking, into Johann's face. The puppy yawned, showing his pink tongue and small white teeth. Then he whined and stumbled about in the basket Johann had bought to transport him in. He could not climb out over its sides, not even in the quiet wayside inns where he and the servant stayed two nights on their long journey.

"*Nein, nein, pudelhund!*" Johann would tell him, laughing at his frantic efforts in both coach and inn chamber to scramble out of his basket. The old man never took him up, though, into his cloak-covered lap as the puppy wished. "I am not to be your master, little one. The baron would part with only a young pup. He insisted that no one but your real master should befriend you. You will see him soon, though. *He* is a *prince!* I am but a servant!"

In the middle of the afternoon of the third day the coach came at last to Linz. Its iron-covered wheels groaned and shrieked across the cobblestone streets. The harsh sounds awakened the puppy whose ears were hurt by them. He howled and went on howling while the coach passed through the city and climbed the hill where the castle stood on a rock over the Danube, green-gray far below.

Johann pulled back the leather curtain nearest him and looked out the coach window at the gray castle, towering high above on the Schlossberg. The castle was constructed of stone and mortar and was not old; yet ivy was slowly covering its walls. Someday it would be only a green bulk against the sky.

Musketeers in scarlet baldrics challenged the coach at the postern gate. Johann showed their captain the letter the Earl of Arundel had sent his master and which he was to deliver to Graf von Kuffstein, the governor of the castle. A good soldier, trained never to show surprise, the captain after reading the letter immediately took out the basket, puppy and all. He peeked once at the dog, then said, "Follow me. I will conduct you to Graf von Kuffstein."

Paying no heed to the poodle, which lay quiet, the musketeer officer led old Johann, who panted soon for breath, up and up flights of steps. The soldier did not seem to see how curiously the little white dog stared up at his great black hat and large blond moustache.

Graf von Kuffstein was a heavyset man with long, gray-streaked fair hair. He sat in a small tapestry-hung stone chamber, a book in his hands. His thirteen-year-old daughter, Susanne Marie, sat across from him. Her dress was of pale blue silk, her eyes a much brighter blue, and her hair dressed in long pale-gold curls.

"*Excellenz*," the musketeer captain bowed, the gold embroidery on his baldric catching the light from the hearth-fire in the chilly room. "I have brought someone to speak with you. He has a letter for you."

Von Kuffstein glanced first at Johann, then in curiosity at the basket the musketeer held. "Give me the letter," he said, stretching out his hand.

The musketeer gave the castle warder the letter. Von Kuffstein read it swiftly, laughed, and then passed it to his daughter. "There is a *pudelhund* in the basket," he told the girl. "Take a look, if you wish." The count spoke to Johann. "The dog is to be a gift for my prisoner, Prince Rupert, eh?"

The count was not an unkind man, and he had become fond of his young charge in the time Rupert had been at Linz. In fact, von Kuffstein felt rather sorry for him al-though the Prince was considered an enemy of Austria. Rupert's father, Frederick, had held the throne of Bohemia, which the Austrian emperor had also claimed. Frederick was now dead, but Rupert's mother was living in exile in the Netherlands, dependent on the charity of the Dutch prince, her kinsman.

Johann bowed deeply and answered the count's ques-tion. "The Earl of Arundel has sent the dog, *Excellenz*. Not long past he was at Vienna as the ambassador of the English king."

Susanne Marie, who had gone to take the basket from

the musketeer, already had the tiny dog in her arms. "Papa, he is a wonderful *pudelhund!*"

The dog liked the girl. He liked her not only because she had picked him up but because of her scent of spice and roses. He licked her on the cheek, and she permitted it, laughing. "Papa, where am I to find Rupert?"

"At this hour he walks in the garden." Von Kuffstein smiled slightly. "Do not pretend to me that you do not know this. You are often enough with him. Since he has become my charge, your mother and I scarcely see you anymore."

"Then, with your permission, I'll take the Englishman's gift to him, Father?" Her voice was teasing. "Such a large savage beast he is, Father!"

Graf von Kuffstein nodded his assent. His daughter took up the basket too now and at once left the room, the puppy still in her arms. *"Pauvre petit,"* she told the dog in French. "I wonder what language Rupert will use to speak to you. What a mixture he uses to me—German, French, and sometimes even Dutch. How it annoys me, but I think he isn't aware of doing it. I wonder what he will call you, my little one?" Her gay face sobered for an instant. An on-looker would have thought her older than thirteen. "I won-der if he'll even want you! He does not seem to need either people or things. Once he trained a hare to follow him like a dog but, then, suddenly he set it free." She began to laugh again. "But if Rupert will not have you, I'll have you! My father would permit it."

The gardens of Linz Castle were not very large, but there were many trees in them, tall ones, firs, oaks, and chestnuts, which shaded the paths among the shrubs clipped into fantastic shapes. Susanne Marie had little diffi- culty finding Rupert. She looked first for musketeer guards, stationed along the garden wall. Where they were, Rupert, the captive, would be!

The Prince sat on a marble bench, a piece of charcoal in his hand, as he sketched the head of a statue across the garden. Rupert arose when he saw the girl coming toward him along the path. He bowed to her. He was well over six feet tall. His face was swarthy and oval, his eyes very dark brown, and the hair that fell to his shoulders black. His coat and breeches were of dark green silk, his shoe buckles of silver. Although his clothing was fine, a close inspection would have betrayed the fact that it was not new.

"What do you have there, my lady?" The young man's voice was low and pleasant to hear.

"Here, take him!" Susanne Marie cried out. " 'Tis a gift, a gift from England! No—not truly from England!" Graf von Kuffstein's daughter showed her confusion. She was often nonplussed by her father's tall prisoner and by his seriousness. He was no gallant as were so many of the Aus- trian soldiers who had come to Linz to visit her father. He seldom smiled and he never paid her or her mother compli- ments—not even at the table on the occasions when he was invited to dine with the family. Now she said, trying to explain, "The dog has been brought to you from Vienna. He is one of Baron von Furstenberg's famous *pudelhunde!*"

Rupert seemed confused now, too. "Who sends him to me? I do not know a Baron von Furstenberg."

"The Earl of Arundel," said the girl.

Now Rupert did come forward. He took the puppy out of her arms. For a long moment the young man looked down at the dog while it looked up at him. Then, unexpectedly, Susanne Marie heard the prisoner of Linz Castle sigh.

"Ah, Arundel. . . . I have told him in my letters that I cannot leave these gardens. How like him to think a dog would help to fill my days. But this poor puppy—to have to share the life I shall probably lead." Then he laughed, his rare laugh, a sharp one.

"What will you call him?" asked the girl, pleased that the distant Rupert had accepted the *pudelhund* so quickly and so easily.

"Boye. I shall name him Boye. Because he is Arundel's gift to me, he should have an English name. I'll speak to him only in English."

Rupert stroked the white puppy, and the dog shivered with pleasure; then he addressed the puppy in English, a language that Susanne Marie did not know. "You'll be a soldier's dog, my lad," he said, giving his whole attention to the puppy. "Would you like that, Boye?"

That first night Boye slept in his master's castle apart-

ments in the same basket that he'd traveled in. He did not
like it. Half the night he whimpered in distress. Toward
dawn he awakened Rupert with his mournful music.

The Prince opened his bed curtains, came over in his
nightgown and stooped down, candle in his hand, to look at
the dog. Rupert spoke to him softly, "What ails you? You do
not like your basket eh? You find it a prison?" He picked up
the poodle and tucked him under his arm, then went to sit
on top of the tall featherbed.

Boye liked this. He liked the scent of his master. Rupert
smelled of tobacco, a pleasant smell. After comforting the
puppy for a time Rupert yawned. He put the dog down on
the floor. "Go, Boye. Explore my prison," the young man
told the poodle. " 'Tis not much to my liking, but you might
find it somewhat more spacious than I." He laughed. "I need
not concern myself with the thought that you might lose
yourself. My doors are locked. Austrian soldiers stand behind them. Good night, Boye." With these words Rupert
folded himself into the feather coverlets.

The floor was icy cold though it was springtime. Over-
joyed to be out of his hated basket at last, the white puppy
went across the floor with his strange, waddling gait. Unsteadily he went from corner to corner, sniffing. He stuck his
nose into everything he could reach, the wide-open ward-
robe, under the carved chests, and even into his master's
shoes. He nosed into every crack and cranny of the bed-
chamber, then moved, a fat white ball on four stout legs,

into Rupert's small audience chamber. It had nothing in it save a table, four chairs, and another chest. There was not one scrap of food there on the floor. This room was of little interest to the dog. Back to the bedchamber went the poodle. This is where the fine-scented man was. This is where the dog meant to be.

Rupert was asleep by now. Boye's thorough tour of inspection had taken two hours. He was lonely again. He tried to rouse the Prince, by barking, then by howling, but Rupert would not awaken. No amount of struggling, trying to climb up onto the featherbed was successful. It was far too slippery. At last the dog gave up. A fold of coverlet, a thick feather-stuffed fold, had slipped down onto the floor. It was most enticing. Boye went to it, curled up on it, sheltered from the cold wooden floor, and finally went to sleep.

When Rupert awoke, he looked at once for Arundel's gift. There on the floor he found him. The Prince smiled and carefully, very carefully, left his bed so as not to disturb the dog. "Some day, God willing, I'll be taking you to England with me," he told the sleeping puppy. "I'll display you to Lord Arundel and see what he thinks of you. Today I'll write him my thanks."

The slow months passed—usually happily for the white dog. The poodle, because he had not yet known anything else, did not fret at his captivity. He was too busy growing and getting to know his master. Boye was far more content at Linz Castle than was the Prince. Sometimes far into the night Rupert paced through his two chambers. Hour after hour he walked when his black moods came upon him. Boye, made nervous by this, walked back and forth, back and forth with him, whining until his master came to a halt at last.

"Go, Boye, go, lie down!" Rupert would then tell him with a laugh. "Do not worry. Soon I'll come to bed." Often the young man then sat down to take up his pipe, pour himself a cup of wine, and begin to read one of von Kuffstein's many books. Boye would sit beside him, happy once more, waiting until his master went to bed for the night.

The dog knew that he was loved by the strange dark man, though Rupert showed his affection in odd ways. His caresses were rough soldier's caresses and his words of endearment came seldom—once Boye was no longer a tiny puppy. The dog seemed to understand the man.

Susanne Marie was very affectionate toward the poodle. She brought Boye tidbits from the castle kitchens, and at table, when the Prince was invited, she fed the dog from her plate. Boye's manners were fine. Rupert had taught him sternly and had permitted no disobedience from his "soldier's dog." The poodle did not put his paws onto the girl's full satin skirts nor did he snap at what she gave him, as her father's hunting dogs did. Because Susanne Marie now wanted a dog, too, Graf von Kuffstein had had a dog brought from Vienna for her, a small gray whippet. She named it Liebling. It was always with her.

Boye tolerated Liebling. To amuse Susanne Marie he

sometimes condescended to chase the whippet in the gardens, but he didn't much enjoy the company of the other dog. Liebling yelped and sometimes she nipped at her mistress and the musketeers. Boye did none of these rude things. Always he kept his dignity. Sometimes this trait of his irked von Kuffstein's daughter, and she would scold him. "You are like unto your master. He is as little civil as you are!"

Rupert, who was meant to hear this, would smile. Once he told her, "He is to be a soldier's dog, my lady. Would you have me forget this? I have had news from my mother in the Netherlands. My uncle, King Charles of England, sends men to Vienna to urge the emperor to free me. Do not seek to make Boye into a lady's dog. I think he'll someday go to war."

Susanne Marie's face fell. She reached down. Her hand lay empty of food, but open toward the poodle. Sensing her quick unhappiness he moved forward, putting his muzzle into her palm. "I do not want you to go to war, Boye," she told the dog, patting the top of his head. The dog understood her mournful tone, if not the words. She looked at Rupert, who sat across from her. "If you are freed, Rupert, you will fight against the emperor again, against Austria?"

"Yes," agreed the somber Prince. "Perhaps I shall. . . . If I do not go to England."

"To England?" asked the girl, surprised. "There is no war in England."

Later Rupert was sketching in the garden and the girl sat near him. The Prince's model was Liebling, who lay under a bush asleep. Rupert said, "I've had a letter from the Earl of Arundel. A courier brought it this morning." He nodded his head toward Boye. "You remember, my lady? He is the Englishman who sent my dog to me. It seems there is a war. The English fight against the Scots. Arundel says there is also other trouble brewing in England. The Parlia' ment in London quarrels with my uncle, the King. Arundel writes that my uncle has need of soldiers, soldiers who have had experience of war. I am a soldier. When I was fourteen years of age, I first went to war. Willingly my mother sent me!" Rupert sighed and Boye came, leaving Susanne Marie, to rest his head on his master's knee and gaze up at him. When his master sighed, the white dog often came to him though he'd not understood the German or French words the young man had said to any of the castle folk.

Chapter **II**

Hugh Joliffe

THROUGHOUT LATE 1639 and 1640 Boye's life was a very changeable one, although his master, Prince Rupert, was still a prisoner of Graf von Kuffstein. Agents from England worked hard at the court of the emperor in Austria trying in vain to have the soldier-nephew of the King of England freed. Rupert had one enemy, a very powerful one, a German duke. The duke once persuaded the emperor to make Rupert's imprisonment more harsh. So for a time Rupert was confined to his small apartments. Twelve musketeers, with swords at their sides, guarded him night and day. Now when Boye was exercised in the gardens, he was taken out on a leash by a musketeer. Though the musketeers were never cruel to him and did not jerk at his collar, Boye disliked them. One or two attempted to pet him and he suffered them to do so, but they well knew he did not enjoy their attentions. Finally when they came to fetch him from his master, he lay down on his belly and forced them to drag him out. After this, he was permitted to stay confined with Rupert. The dog joined the young man in walking back and forth, back and forth.

Susanne Marie was furiously angry at the orders the emperor had sent her father, thanks to the ill will of the duke, who saw the soldier Rupert as a dangerous enemy. She ranted at her father, then pleaded with him, and finally got him to relax his rules again—when the duke went back to Bavaria. Thanks to these two things, Rupert's and Boye's lives became easier.

Some of the Austrian nobles had disapproved of the duke's harshness toward the young prisoner. They were also fascinated by his reputation as a soldier. As soldiers themselves, men who had fought against him, they admired him for his bravery and daring. Above all, they found him very young for the military successes he had won while fighting for his father's claim to the throne of Bohemia. Because they wanted to know him better, the Prince, although under heavy guard, was now permitted to leave Linz Castle and to accept their invitations to hunt with them. Boye sometimes went along in the coach that took his master. How the white dog loved these excursions into the outside world! How he loved going out of Linz by its great gates.

Deer were found everywhere in forested western Austria—as were hares. Often Boye hunted with Rupert and with his master's hosts. He proved to be a worthy hunter and a natural retriever. Most of all he liked retrieving water-fowl. Like all poodles, he was a true water dog. Nothing gave him more happiness than leaping into the Danube or a smaller stream, swimming after a wild duck. But he enjoyed almost as much sitting silently beside his master while Rupert fished in the river above Linz for huchen, trout, and grayling.

Graf von Kuffstein was also a fisherman and hunter. He and Susanne Marie sat with the Prince one gray spring morning of 1641. Each had a fishing rod in hand. Each was supremely content. Lying not far from the count, on his haunches, his large head on his paws, was Boye, also very content. Boye now knew better than to try to retrieve fish his master had caught. Hare and birds were fine, not fish. One warning shout from the Prince some months past had taught him that fact when he had first belly-landed in the water to bring home the fish his master had caught. Rupert feared the hook. When it had been shown to Boye, so did the intelligent dog.

"*Ach,*" remarked von Kuffstein now to his prisoner. "Your *pudelhund* grows uncommonly large. They tell me he eats as much meat in one day as two of my musketeers. The beef and vension he devours! I hear that he pulled down a stag, Your Highness, when last you hunted with him. I was told Baron von Furstenberg was there and was delighted to see this because the feat honored his breed of dogs."

"It was not a *large* stag!" Rupert said with a smile.

"No matter," von Kuffstein told him. "Few dogs can do that. You go boar hunting next week, I'm told, at the invitation of the emperor's cousin. Will you take your dog?"

Rupert looked over his shoulder at Boye. "No, Graf von Kuffstein, I think not. A wild boar is a very dangerous animal. What if Boye should attempt to pull him down? I find it difficult now to hold him back. A boar's tusks are cruel."

Von Kuffstein nodded agreement. "So are a stag's horns. Well, then, my daughter and I will look after him—or perhaps the lad will see to his welfare while you are gone? That should be one of his duties, I suppose?"

"Lad?" asked Rupert quickly, catching the unexplained word. "What lad do you speak of?"

"The boy you are to be sent from England. The emperor allows you a serving lad now—a page. The English ambassador at Vienna has written me this. He is to be either a Dutch or an English lad."

Von Kuffstein's daughter broke in, crying out, "Papa, you've given away the surprise! He was not to know—not until the lad arrives." Her angry words affected Liebling, who set up a yapping that hurt Boye's ears. Boye growled deep in his throat at the whippet, who gave him one look and then fell silent, to Graf von Kuffstein's amusement.

"When shall he come here?" Rupert asked, when the yapping had ceased.

"On the morrow," replied von Kuffstein.

Boye went to the castle tennis court with his master the next morning, although he hated to watch the game. The bouncing ball maddened him. He could not help but follow it with his eyes while his master stubbornly sent it back and forth over a net and a musketeer on the other side whacked the ball back to Rupert. It had not been easy for Rupert to break his poodle of the habit of leaping up, catching the ball on its first bounce, and running off with it. This happened time and time again. Both his master and the musketeers who played against the Prince ran cursing after Boye for days, swatting at him with the racquets as the dog led them a chase through the shrubbery, around trees, and along the garden paths. Susanne Marie enjoyed Boye's variation on the game and applauded wildly, laughing, when Liebling joined in the chase. But at last Rupert had made Boye understand that tennis was for men, not for poodles. Consequently Boye detested the game.

This particular morning Boye was morose. He lay on the grass beside Graf von Kuffstein's daughter, who read a book because she also disliked tennis.

This is where the poodle was when a musketeer arrived with a lad in tow, a lad in a long gray cloak. As he did with all newcomers, rarities at Linz Castle, Boye got up and slowly came forward to inspect him.

The lad was about eleven years old. His long curling hair was golden-brown, his round eyes a beautiful shade of violet-blue. His face was heart shaped and pale as an ivory statue. He wore black beneath his gray cloak, pure black from his broad hat to his traveling boots. Black became his paleness marvelously well.

Susanne Marie von Kuffstein and the Prince saw him at the same moment, some seconds after Boye, who had heard the footsteps. The girl put down her book, arose, and shook wide her apricot-colored skirts. Liebling came out from under her bench while Rupert made a signal to his musketeer opponent to wait before he sent the ball back.

The boy came forward, took off his hat, and held it before his breast, then bowed. His voice was high and clear and his words in English. "Your Highness, I am named Hugh Joliffe. I am dispatched to serve you."

"An English lad then?" Rupert seemed pleased. He spoke to Susanne Marie in German. "It is what I would have chosen—a boy who has come from England."

"And such a pretty lad!" exclaimed von Kuffstein's daughter. "Come, Boye," she called. She motioned for the poodle to go greet the boy, who stood motionless with his hat over his breast.

For a long, a very long moment, the dog and Hugh Joliffe looked at one another. There was at first no expression on the face of the remarkably handsome boy; then he looked up to give the Prince an angel's smile. Liebling ran to him, leaped up on him, and barked.

Boye's behavior was much different from the whippet's. At first, at Susanne's motion, he had come forward, but then all at once, he had stepped back, stiff-legged. The poodle had caught Hugh's scent and had not liked it. His lips had lifted in a silent snarl, a snarl that neither his master nor the girl had seen.

Some days after Hugh Joliffe came to serve him, Rupert rode off boar hunting for a fortnight, leaving Boye alone for the first time with the page. Hugh was not truly unkind to the white dog, but it became at once clear that the boy had no affection for the poodle. He was dutiful in fetching the dog's food from the kitchens and in taking him to the gardens, but like the musketeers who had walked Boye, Hugh had no real interest in the dog.

Boye sensed in his doglike way that there was something awry with his master's page, the lad who never spoke to him or called him by name. There was an odd chill in Hugh's manner. Most folk saw only his handsome face and figure and his dazzling, melting smile. They found him wonderfully polite and well bred and suspected nothing. Because the page presented a pleasant surface, they did not see beneath it.

The white poodle did. Rupert was the exact opposite of Hugh. What lay beneath the soldier's harsh exterior was warm and generous—though few people knew so.

While the Prince was away from Linz Castle Boye

grieved for him. Susanne Marie guessed this from the dog's manner. She, too, missed Rupert. She noticed that the large dog did not whine or whimper when Hugh took him out, although she saw the lad once tug hard at his leash, cutting off the dog's breath for a moment as they went about the castle grounds. The girl could not scold the page because she had no English. She found Hugh's German scant, indeed.

From her father she learned the page's strange history. The lad, like the poodle, had come to Linz from Vienna. His father had been a minor servant attached to the household of the English ambassador, who now dickered with the emperor for Rupert's release. The boy's father had died of a fever in Vienna. Hugh, motherless since birth, had no family in England and the English in Vienna had not known what to do with the orphaned boy. There was no place for him in any of the Viennese households of the English diplomats. They had servants enough. Then the ambassador had bethought himself of the servantless Prince. Here was the perfect opportunity for the orphan. What a remarkably handsome boy he was—remarkably intelligent, too! The ambassador found little difficulty in having Master Joliffe accepted as a page by the emperor, who saw no reason why Rupert could not have a servant.

Susanne Marie had listened very carefully to what her father told her of Hugh; then she said, "Boye does not like the page, Papa."

Graf von Kuffstein had laughed at this. "And what of that? Who knows what a dog is thinking?"

Susanne Marie spoke seriously. "If Boye does not like him, I don't like him. I would warn Rupert of him if I thought he would believe me, but I know he would not. Rupert loves all the English."

For a time Boye tolerated Hugh's treatment of him, but one evening, an evening only three days before the Prince returned to the castle, matters came to a head. The page took a liberty the dog would not permit. For the poodle it was the final outrage.

Hugh had his own small truckle bed in Rupert's bed-chamber, but this night while Rupert was away the boy climbed up onto the great featherbed and lay down as if he meant to sleep there. Boye walked toward him and growled his threats. This was Rupert's bed, the poodle well knew. No one slept there but his master.

Hugh sat in his nightgown, motionless on top of the coverlets, his eyes on the dog. "Get you gone, cur!" he said in a whisper, though because Rupert was gone there were no guards outside the door.

Boye would not leave. He advanced toward the bed, his upper lip lifted in a snarl. Yet Hugh did not get down. Instead he took a pewter candlestick from the table near the bed and lifted it high over his head. From the expression about his eyes and mouth Boye knew Hugh would strike him.

Before he could bring it down, though, on the dog's back or head, the poodle sprang, a white flash, onto the bed. Catching hold of the hem of the linen nightgown with his teeth, Boye hauled at the page, bringing him with a crash down to the floor where in the poodle's judgment he belonged. Hugh's face was scarlet with anger, but he made no outcry. He caught hold of a bedpost and clung to it, his bedgown torn and the poodle, a piece of Hugh's gown still in his jaws, ready for the second attack.

Boye went into a fury now. To his way of thinking the page not only had no right to be on top of the bed, he had no right to be near it. The bed was Rupert's! The truckle bed was the place for Hugh Joliffe. Boye let the bit of linen fall. Swiftly he darted in again and this time sunk his teeth into Hugh's leg above his ankle and hung on.

Not even now did Hugh cry out, but he let go the bedpost and stood away from it. "Get away, cur!" he told Boye. Hugh's tone was icy. Its calm chill reached the dog's awareness as screams and a struggle would not have. The poodle released Hugh Joliffe, but, still snarling, backed away until he stood protectively between the page and his master's bed.

He watched as the lad limped across the chamber and took a handkerchief from the little chest he'd brought with him from Vienna and bandaged his bleeding ankle. He watched, growling, as Hugh went to his truckle bed and lay there propped up on his elbow watching the dog. Boye heard the page's hoarse words, "Someday, cur, I shall kill you. He loves *you* best!"

Hugh Joliffe's black hose covered his bandaged ankle. The page explained his limp by saying he had fallen on the steps leading to his master's apartment. His lie was believed by everyone, for Hugh was clever at keeping his secret. He burned his torn nightgown in the hearthfire and along with it the piece of linen Boye had ripped from it. When the Prince returned, the page showed a careful courtesy to the dog. When Rupert was again away, though, Hugh avoided Boye and often neglected to bring him his food. The cooks of the castle kitchen knew this from the way the white dog hung about the kitchen doors. One of them always fed him when he came and expectantly but politely waited. Before long the poodle learned when he was hungry to summon the kind woman with a soft bark.

Rupert was never aware of Hugh's neglect, thanks to the cook's generosity. He knew only that Boye was healthy and alert and very, very happy to see him when he returned from the hunting lodges where he had been entertained hunting the fierce wild boars of the Austrian forests.

After three years of imprisonment, in late October of 1641, Rupert's dreams of liberty at last came true. The English diplomats King Charles had sent to Vienna to plead for his nephew achieved success. The emperor sent a courier to

Graf von Kuffstein at Linz, telling him to let his prisoner go. With the letter came a safe-conduct, which would permit Rupert, a former enemy soldier, to travel through Austria and Germany.

At once the governor of Linz Castle went to see his prisoner and tell him the good news. "Where will you go, Your Highness?" he asked Rupert over a cup of wine.

"To The Hague." Rupert had been very pleased to hear the long-hoped-for news. Boye had come quickly to him at his first word. Now the Prince sat in his little audience chamber, fondling the poodle's ears, while Hugh stood at his elbow waiting for orders. Rupert's smile had changed to a slight frown when he spoke of the Netherlands city. "I do not know how my mother will receive me on my return. I have had a letter from a friend in England, a letter which you as my jailer must surely have read. In it I was told that when I was captured by the Austrians, my mother said that she would rather I'd been killed than held prisoner."

Graf von Kuffstein looked into his wine cup. He well remembered that letter. The count loved his own tall sons, who now served the emperor in Vienna. The Austrian nobleman could not understand the Queen of Bohemia. She must be a madwoman, he told himself, not to love her soldier son, for all his somber temperament.

"I wish you well in your freedom, Your Highness. You will serve as a soldier again, of course?"

"I know no other thing well." Rupert's smile was a

twisted one. "If I were not a prince, I would become a limner, but such things are not for princes." Rupert turned his head to look at Hugh. "I shall send you back to Vienna to the ambassador's house, Hugh. I will send what money I can with you. The ambassador will find you a new master. Graf von Kuffstein, I am sure, can give you a horse from his stables, and you will travel there with the courier who has brought me news of my freedom." The Prince went on more slowly, "I regret I cannot take you to The Hague with me, lad. The journey is long and my welcome there somewhat uncertain."

Not one flicker of expression had crossed the English boy's face when he heard the news that he was to return to Vienna. He only shot a glance toward Boye, then looked back to his master. "What will you do with *him*, master?" he said, pointing to the dog.

"My dog?" Rupert seemed surprised by the question. "He has been with me since he was a puppy. Boye comes to the Netherlands. He is fully grown now. I hope soon to take him along to England."

Hugh burst out with, "Someday soon, Your Highness, I shall be full grown, too! Then I shall come to England. I shall seek you out to serve you again. Will you have me?" His words were said in a manner that was fierce, a manner totally strange to him.

Both Graf von Kuffstein and the Prince looked at him in surprise. Rupert nodded. "To be sure, lad, I'll have you. You've served me well when I was a prisoner. That cannot have been easy for you. How could I deny your request when I am a free man?"

"Would you have more wine now?" asked the page. Hugh at once recovered his poise at his master's promise. He poured each man more wine. Then he stood behind the Prince, looking out with venom from under his half-closed eyelids at the white poodle who would leave Austria with Rupert when he was forced to stay behind.

Boye was not aware of how Hugh Joliffe, who had been dismissed, stared at him. The poodle leaned contentedly against his master's knee. The dog had understood very well the words *Boye comes!* These were the two words he loved best. Even if he had been human and could have understood what Hugh had said, he would not have concerned himself with the page's words—no more than Rupert, himself, did. The Hague was many leagues to the north and west of Austria. England lay even farther away. As Rupert did not, no one would have really thought that the page could ever make his way to England from Vienna.

Neither man realized what the page was saying to himself. "I *will* find the Prince in England someday! He is a master other serving lads will envy. Few boys have the luck to serve a Prince. I'll have the ambassador send me to England somehow—as soon as I can. King Charles's best-loved nephew should not be difficult to find. The ambassador's other servants shall not laugh long at *me* in Vienna.

"Someday, in England, I'll kill this Austrian cur who has bitten me! Then the Prince will love *me* best."

Chapter III

The Queen of Bohemia

RUPERT HAD THOUGHT of journeying to the Netherlands through France, which he considered the safest way of all, but he changed his mind. Instead he decided to visit Prague, the city where he had been born, the city where his father had once and only briefly been a king. He did not remember Prague because he had been forced to flee it as an infant, but it held glories for him yet.

Although he was not wearied by the trip, Boye was confused by such a long period of travel. He had never gone half so far before. He found the coach the Austrian emperor had put at his master's convenience uncomfortable. Its floor was cold, its leather seat very slippery. He did not like snow-covered Prague, and he missed the castle cook's tidbits at the door. Rupert did not seem to care when and what he ate. This was not true of the poodle.

The cheapest, easiest way to travel to the Netherlands was by river, so after a brief stop in Saxony in Germany, Rupert and Boye went overland by common coach across Thuringia and Hesse until they reached the Rhine River at Bonn. Because they had very little money now, Rupert and Boye ate sparingly. Boye was pleased when they took ship at Bonn; on the ship they dined better with the fat captain.

On the nineteenth of December the two travelers were at last put ashore in the Dutch city of Rotterdam. "We are nearly home now, Boye," Rupert told his dog. Rupert was lean and weary while Boye was as gaunt as his master. Because the Prince had known they would be traveling in chill weather, he had not had Boye clipped before they set out. "You have the look of a sheep about you—an unsheared one," the Prince told the poodle with a laugh as they left the wharves and went into Rotterdam.

The Prince's odd appearance, his swarthy skin, black hair, and shabby cloak attracted the attention of the red-cheeked Dutch. Some men and boys in heavy dark cloaks and wooden clogs stopped to listen curiously to the tall, young, foreign-looking man with the large dog. Some of the boys followed him and Boye to a tavern in the center of the city.

Rupert stopped there and addressed Boye once more, "You and I shall have an excellent supper here. Then we'll take a coach to The Hague on the morrow. 'Tis not far. Are you as weary as I am of coaches, decks, and cabins, Boye?"

A plump Dutch youth spoke loudly and scornfully to the others with him. He had heard English sailors speak and understood enough of the words to make out the tongue Rupert spoke. In Dutch he said to his companions, "An Englisher! These Englishers are mad. They speak to dogs and horses!"

"Indeed the Englishers do! Dogs and horses do not make rude replies," commented Rupert, who now swung around to address the boys in Dutch. He enjoyed their looks of surprise, laughed once, and went into the tavern.

After a dinner of fish and good wine from Spain for Rupert and a great hunk of mutton for Boye, the Prince called for a pair of shears. By the light of the tavern hearth-fire and two candles he clipped the hair that hung down over Boye's eyes. "Now," announced the poodle's master, "you will be able to see my loving mother and she—you."

They slept that night in the tavern. The next morning during a gentle snowstorm Rupert took a coach northwest-ward to The Hague. The driver had not wanted to permit the poodle inside the coach, but when Rupert had given him his last florin and put his hand to the hilt of his sword, the Dutchman had agreed. So Boye rode at Rupert's feet for a time; then, when a fat burgher alighted south of Delft be-side his windmill and farm, the shivering dog leaped up onto the seat and slept beside his half-asleep and also shiver-ing master. The snowstorm had grown heavier while the

coach jolted over the frozen puddles and ruts. Because of
the drawn leather curtains, Boye could not stick his head
out as usual to see the countryside, but as they traveled a
new scent came ever stronger to him.

He lifted his nose and sniffed it. Then he leaned on his
master until he awakened him. Rupert saw how the poodle
snuffled now. "No, Boye," he told him, " 'tis not fish in some
burgher's basket in the coach you scent. 'Tis the sea!" He
patted the dog's head. "I forget. You've not seen the sea,
have you? It differs somewhat from the Danube and the
Rhine."

In the evening they arrived at last at The Hague and,
half-frozen, got stiffly down out of the coach. The man and
the dog stood for a moment, snowflakes falling about them,
lighting softly on the poodle's inquisitive nose. There was no
one to greet them. Rupert spoke to Boye again. "I do not
think we are expected here in the Netherlands. No one recognized me in Rotterdam, a place I've often been." The
Prince touched the dog's back. "We'll make our way to the
Voorhout on foot. 'Tis where my mother lives. If we are not
expected, why should we hurry, lad?"

The Hague was silent this snowy night. Because of the
bitter cold few people were about. The two were not
marked out as they walked across the brick streets except as
a very thin, very tall young man and a large white dog. The
Voorhout was a most fashionable section of The Hague. The
Stadtholder of the Netherlands was a most generous host to

the exiled Queen of Bohemia. He gave the widow Queen two fine houses there. It was to the larger one, a brick house with four gables, that Rupert and the poodle made their way.

"Are you hungry, Boye?" the Prince asked the dog.

Boye knew the word *hungry*. He pressed close to his master and looked longingly up at him. Hungry or no, he was with Rupert, but the truth of the matter was that the dog was famished.

Rupert smiled and touched Boye's head. "We are here." He gripped the dog's collar, sighed, and went up the steps. The Prince lifted the knocker and slammed it onto the door.

A tall servant boy in popinjay green livery came to the door. He stared at Rupert over the candle he held and his jaw dropped. "Your Highness!" he exclaimed in English.

"Aye," Rupert told him. "I have returned." His hand still on Boye's collar, he shouldered his way past the serv' ant. "Would you inform Her Majesty, my mother, that I have come home?"

"At once! At once!" the servant told the Prince, and he was gone down a long dark passageway. Rupert, the dog at his heels, followed his light.

Boye sniffed the closed warm air of the house. He smelled strange scents, rare spices he had never smelled be' fore. Bright'colored carpets beneath his paws were very soft, and the furniture in the passageway tall, heavy, and dark. He did not know how prosperous the Netherlands was or how great its trade with the East Indies, the Spice Islands. To him the passageway was strange. He would have liked to nose about, but his master held him fast. He had caught other scents now beside those of spices. One was definitely of dogs, but there was another scent, too, a sharp unpleasant one of some other animal—a strange animal. He did not like the smell. He whined and tried to tug loose, but Rupert murmured to him, "Stay—stay, Boye!"

At last the servant led them into a low-ceilinged wood-paneled chamber where five people sat at supper, each with a liveried manservant behind his chair. There were three girls, two dark, one fair haired. At the head of the table sat a plump woman with graying blond hair, a woman who wore a satin gown of emerald green. On her right sat a small man in a black brocade coat. All five raised their heads from their supper to stare at the unsummoned servant lad and then to gape first at Rupert, then at Boye.

Rupert bowed gravely to his mother, the Queen of Bohemia, then to his three sisters present. For the youngest, dark-haired Sophie, he had a quick, flashing smile. Last of all the Prince bowed to the man in black, his mother's wealthy English friend, a family benefactor.

There was a silence for a time, a silence that no person broke. A dog's growl arose to break it, and it was not a growl from Boye who stood rigid beside his master, sniffing the air of the room, which smelled very strongly of dogs.

Another dog, a large brown animal with pricked ears, came out from under the tablecovering. He slunk toward the poodle. Behind him came still another dog, a small spaniel, also growling. The hair rose on Boye's back as he tensed himself.

"I see you have dogs still, my mother?" Rupert said calmly, taking a firmer grip on his poodle.

"And I see you have a dog also?" remarked the Queen of Bohemia, just as calmly. She clapped her hands and her dogs retreated back under the table. "Rupert, we did not know you had been set free!" She laughed. "I suppose I shall receive the message tomorrow that Rupert the Devil is coming home. Come, kiss me! Let me look at you."

The Prince crossed the room, kissed his mother on the cheek, and stood before her to be inspected. Boye had come with him. He was still nervous. He kept his eye on the table-cloth under which the dogs lurked, not looking at the Queen of Bohemia. All the same he was very aware of her perfume, a musky heavy one.

"You are very thin," the Queen told her son. She examined Boye, too, with her bright gaze and laughed. "And your dog is also thin. That is shameful—that he be gaunt! Did they never feed him or, for that matter, you in Austria? Sit down." She addressed the servant behind her. "Serve my son his supper. Then fetch this dog food, too—a great bowl of it. I cannot abide seeing thin beasts!"

Rupert grinned at Sophie again. Seating himself with

Boye beside him, he told the poodle, "Lie down, Boye." Boye sank to his belly as close as possible to his master's chair while the Prince spoke with his family and his mother's English friend of his long journey. Boye could see under the table. There lay the Queen's dogs, their eyes steady on the stranger. One of them showed his teeth in a silent snarl, and Boye felt an answering growl rise in his throat, but at his first sound his master's hand was on his back, restraining him.

When the bowl of cut-up meat was brought him, Boye stood warily over it, gulping it down while his master above also stuffed himself with food. The poodle heard the babble of voices over him, gay and lively voices. Still he did not take his eyes from the Queen's dogs who he thought might attack him at any moment and eat his food.

Over his head the Queen of Bohemia said, "Rupert, what am I to do with you? There is nothing here for you in the Netherlands. You are a soldier. We are not at war, though the Stadtholder will be happy to see you, of course. I'll send a dispatch tomorrow to England to your uncle, telling him you are safely here. Perhaps he can find employment for your sword?"

The English lord in black spoke in his slow fashion. "Your Majesty, there is a revolt against England in Ireland now. The Prince might go there to serve in King Charles's army."

Rupert spoke to Boye, who had finished his food and

who was still cautiously watching the other dogs. "Would you like that, Boye? Do you want to go to Ireland to put down a revolt? Ireland is not far from England."

The dog caught the eagerness in his master's tone. Rupert had sounded pleased. What made Rupert happy, made Boye happy. The poodle lay down again, still keeping a weather eye on the Queen's dogs who had now lost interest in him and gone to sleep, snoring, next to the Queen's feet. Boye was almost content except for that strange, sharp odor that now and again came to his nostrils and made him want to sneeze. *What* was it, he wanted to know? Rupert saw him crinkle his nose again and again as he lifted his head. The Prince smiled, knowing full well what it was Boye smelled.

The Queen, her daughters, and the Englishman got up at last and went to her audience chamber, down another passageway. This was a large chilly room, but at one end a fire blazed in the great hearth. Before it, away from the ice-patterned windows, a number of chairs had been placed. One of them was velvet-upholstered with a high back, the Queen's chair.

Boye's nose, then his eyes, soon became aware of something strange—the number of animals in the chamber. The Queen's two "supper" dogs had come with her at her heels as she led the way out of the smaller room. In addition, ten more dogs, dogs of all sizes and breeds, lay basking in the warmth of the hearthfire. The scent of dog was very powerful now—yet overriding it was the peculiar odor that had bedeviled the poodle ever since he had entered this house.

One of the audience-chamber dogs spotted the white newcomer. He got up and yelped a warning. This brought the others to their feet, too. They all came slowly forward in a pack to inspect the interloper. The yelp had also brought "other things" to an interest in the two new arrivals, Rupert and Boye. One of these "other things" jumped down from the arm of the Queen's chair. Another sat on its top while three others were perched on the mantelpiece, picking at each other's fur.

Boye had never seen such creatures before, but he knew at once that they were the source of the wretched smell. What horrible things they were! One of them came running across the floor toward him, walking upright the way a man walked. The poodle snarled, then barked, and frantically tried to twist away from his master.

"No, Boye, no! 'Tis naught but a monkey!" Rupert told him, struggling to hold him.

The first monkey, with the second at his tail, stopped before the poodle. A lean thing of brown-black fur he stood up and glared with wicked little black eyes at Boye. His mouth opened and his tiny yellow teeth showed as he chattered, leaping up and down, scolding. Then this evil-smelling monkey did an outrageous thing. While the Queen's dogs set up a din of howling and barking and the monkey's fellows, horrid duplicates of himself, shrieked and chattered, the first monkey jumped up onto the poodle's back. He gripped Boye's heavy mane of hair in his strong little paws, hurting the dog.

Rupert could not restrain the half-mad poodle any longer. With the monkey riding him, Boye broke loose. Enraged by the monkey's behavior, Boye charged around and around the large chamber. The twelve dogs and the other four monkeys joined in the noisy frantic chase. No matter how he tried, not even by lying down and rolling around while snapping at it, could Boye dislodge the monkey. The poodle did not hear Rupert's shouts "Come, Boye!" He did not hear the laughter of the Queen or of her daughters. He heard only the cries of the pack of animals that hunted him and knew only that somehow he must rid himself of this dreadful thing that rode him.

It was Rupert's youngest sister who saved Boye. Sophie waded into the swarm of animals. She plucked the poodle's unwelcome rider from his back, spanked it, put it onto her shoulder, and marched to her chair and sat down. "It is no way to greet a guest!" she declared in a high, riding voice.

Boye stood, his sides heaving with terror and fatigue, while the noise subsided at last. Then, at the Prince's command, he came to him and sat beside him, shivering. "Thank you, my lady," Rupert said to his little sister as gravely as if she had been an adult.

Sophie nodded. "You have brought a very fine dog with you," she told him. "What is he named? How did you come by him?"

"He is named Boye."

"That is an *English* name for an *Austrian* dog," commented the little girl in the oyster-hued satin gown. "I do not like the name. Soldiers have no imagination. I would have called him something mighty."

"Aye, his name is English. That is because he will go to England with me, my lady. I am sorry that you are not pleased with his name, but he has had it for some years and has become accustomed to it. I have raised him as an English dog. If you are to command him, you must speak English to him—not French or Dutch or German—as you speak to your sisters and to me and my other brothers. Boye is to be a soldier's dog!"

"Ah—Rupert the Devil's dog!" put in the Queen of Bohemia. "Rupert, if your dog cannot face cannon and swords better than he has faced my monkey Sweeting"—here she fed the monkey who had ridden on the poodle a bit of candied fruit—"he will never be a soldier's dog."

"He does not fear the crackling of the arquebus, and he is a fearless hunter, Mother!"

The Queen shrugged her shoulders. " 'Tis of no matter truly. Rupert, you are as ill-bred as ever, I think. That is what comes of spending your time always with soldiers. Tell your sister how you came by this animal, my Sweeting's courser?"

Then, while they all listened, the Prince told them of the Earl of Arundel's gift. Because they seemed still interested, he also spoke of the English page sent him from

Vienna and of Hugh's statement that he would seek Rupert
out again in England.

All but Sophie laughed to hear this. She said soberly, "I
think he *will* come to you, my brother," but her words were
greeted only with more laughter.

After a time Boye grew calm. He lay close beside his
master, not far from the hearthplace but far enough from
the other dogs. He enjoyed the warmth as well as his full
stomach. His eyes, however, did not leave the Queen, who
sat surrounded by her camp of dogs and her monkeys.
Whatever happened, that monkey the Queen fed sweetmeats constantly to was not to approach him again!

The poodle hated monkeys!

The Queen of Bohemia's daughters lived with her; her
sons did not. They had separate establishments in The
Hague.

Boye and his master went to live with Maurice, Rupert's younger brother.

"Now I wonder if you and Maurice will be happy together?" Rupert told the poodle laughingly as they set out
later that snowy night. "My mother has been known to
speak of him as yet another of her monkeys! But I will tell
you this, Maurice is my favorite brother. I do not love the
others half so well."

Maurice kept his lodgings, and poor lodgings they
were, on the second floor of an old Dutch house. Boye did

not like them. They smelled of mice, and the noises from the people who lived above and below annoyed him, but he took to Maurice himself, at once.

Rupert's next youngest brother was lying on his bed, smoking his pipe, blowing rings into the air, when Rupert, without knocking, came in. "Damme, you're back," was Maurice's first statement. "I told our mother the Austrians could not contain you long!" He got up easily, put down his pipe, and embraced his brother. Although shorter, he resembled Rupert.

Maurice gazed at Boye. "What is that you've brought with you, Rupert—a sheep?"

"I call him Boye! He is not well clipped," replied Rupert with a smile. "He is a *pudelhund* from Austria, a gift of Arundel."

"Um-m" said Maurice, who sat down on his bed again and whistled softly.

At Rupert's encouraging nudge Boye came forward to sniff Maurice's outstretched hand as the younger prince stayed motionless.

Boye liked Maurice's interesting scent of tobacco and dogs and horses. He approved. There was no detestable odor of monkey about him at all. The poodle moved closer and permitted Maurice, who sighed, to fondle his mane.

"He is a fine beauty," Maurice told his brother. "I have no dogs now. My mother's twelve curs are enough for one family. Will you keep your dog?"

Rupert nodded. "Boye will stay with me—or with us."

Maurice's grin was a quick one. "For you and for your *pudelhund,* or whatever he is called, I'll make my exceptions. You will live here with me—both of you!" The younger prince tugged one of Boye's ears. "So I will not have another dog. I do not think this one of yours would permit it."

Rupert sat down on the sagging bed, too, then stared up at its faded red hangings. "I do not think Boye would. If we are to share lodgings, we can share my dog, I think."

"And perhaps a soldier's life together again, eh?" put in Maurice, who displayed the sleeve of his shabby blue velvet coat. "That can't come to me too swiftly, brother!"

Nevertheless, Rupert, Maurice, and Boye were at loose ends for a long time. Although King Charles knew that Rupert was no longer a prisoner, no message that would take him to England came for him. The two young men waited and amused themselves as best they could in the dull little Dutch city. Boye went everywhere with them, running at the heels of their horses when they joined the boring daily promenade along the Voorhout. He accompanied them on the short winter afternoons when they skated on the canals with their sisters and younger brothers.

How Boye loved the canals! He liked to run, then slide on their strange gray-glistening surface, slithering around and around on his tail, barking wildly, while everyone laughed at him. He liked, too, to go to the seashore with Rupert. Once he dashed out into the icy North Sea and found it very little like the Danube. No, he did not choose to retrieve in salt water. It got up a dog's nose and stung.

Best of all, though, the poodle loved the Dutch swans. The birds on the thin-iced Vijver, the dark water before the Buitenhof, were fascinating, yet Boye chased them but once. His first swan battle was his last. He retreated swiftly when an angry, hissing cob came at him with his terrible white wings outspread.

Prince Maurice enjoyed this. He doubled up with laughter and clapped the watching Rupert on the shoulder. Maurice was much less somber than his brother. "You said he was to be a soldier's dog, Rupert? What sort of warrior retreats from a bird?"

"A clever one, I would say," Rupert told Maurice, smiling. "I do not think even Boye could defeat a swan, which can break a man's arm with one blow of its wing."

As the two brothers continued walking, Rupert turned serious. "Our mother has had news from King Charles. There is worse trouble in England. The Parliament is openly attacking our uncle's ministers of state." Rupert called Boye to him. He stooped and patted the dog. "Let the swans be, Boye!" Rupert's eyes were on his brother, though, as he spoke. "It seems I am called to England to see the King." The Prince addressed Boye again. "I shall take you with me, lad. There you may meet the Earl of Arundel, whose gift you were—and the King and Queen of England."

Maurice gazed after the poodle who had gone out onto a frozen canal again to slide about. "I wish I, too, might go to England with you, but I was not asked. You should warn your Austrian dog, Rupert, that English swans are no more friendly than Dutch swans. You should teach him rather to catch the rats and mice that infest our chambers and eat our threadbare breeches. Now there is a chore for your *pudel-hund*. But he thinks himself above rat catching."

Maurice became sober faced, too, now. "Our mother owes money to every man of trade in The Hague. The pension our uncle, King Charles, has promised is not always sent her. We live on the bounty of Dutch and English friends. I am weary of our lodgings, our mother's house, her accursed monkeys, and of the Netherlands. I am weary of Dutch burghers who wear only black. If there was a war somewhere, I would go to it if I had to walk. Like you, Rupert, I know but one thing, a soldier's life. I had hoped to fight for King Charles against the Scots two years past, but that war is ended."

"Aye," commented Prince Rupert bitterly. "What is of less worth than a soldier without employment? I spent too many years a prisoner in Linz. Wars ended during those years. Now I must go in peace to England—and not to war in Ireland at all."

Once he knew that he was to "come" Boye would not

let his master out of his sight for a moment for fear he
would be left behind as he sometimes had been in Austria.
Over and over again Rupert told the dog, "Boye, you *will
come* with me!" Still the poodle followed at his heels like a
white shadow.

At last they left. They crossed the North Sea during
blustery weather so both Prince and dog stayed below
decks. In the English Channel, however, both ventured out
to see a pale gray sky and gray-green water. The Channel
was even rougher than the North Sea. Rupert was seasick.
Boye could scarcely keep his feet on the wildly moving
deck. Yet Rupert would not go below to his little cabin;
Boye, for his part, would not leave the Prince. Finally at the
Prince's command a Dutch sailor tied the dog to the ship's
mast so he would not skid overboard when a high swell hit
the ship and made her lurch. Rupert stayed by him, his
cloak billowing in the wind, his hair blown back from his
dark, eager hawk's face.

"There it is, Boye!" Rupert once shouted aloud to the
poodle. "We are in the Strait of Dover. I remember the great
cliffs of the place. Now, at last, you will see Dover Castle
and England!"

Still shaky from his recent seasickness, Rupert changed
to a new suit of black silk with a lace-trimmed collar and
gold buttons. Somewhere, he didn't know how, his mother
had found the money for it. Boye had been clipped before
they left The Hague so he also was presentable. Rupert well

knew how striking a pair they made, the swarthy man in black and the pure white dog.

The Prince's arrival in England was greeted by a formal salute, the booming of cannon from the castle battlements. As Rupert had said, his dog had heard the sound of musket and arquebus, but this was his first experience with cannon. In the coach King Charles had sent to fetch his nephew to him, the poodle shrank, trembling, toward his master as the cannon thundered over the Strait of Dover. The Prince laughed at him. "If you are to be a soldier's dog—my dog— you will not be frightened by the bellow of the great guns!"

Dover Castle was a large building made of stone, guarded by musketeers and halberdiers. Its cold floors under Boye's paws made him dimly recall Linz Castle, a memory that was fading now. The great number of people, men in magnificent clothing, in the King's antechamber did not make him nervous, though. He had seen many folk at The Hague. He stood quietly by his master as the English courtiers and royal officials flocked around Rupert to speak with him about his release from the Austrians. The dog sniffed their scents and found them proper—tobacco and dogs—not one hint of monkeys.

One of these men attending King Charles was a gray-haired person, somberly garbed in a plain brown silk coat and snuff-colored breeches. Among the rainbow-plumage courtiers at the English court, he seemed ill placed, indeed. He came forward the moment he spied Rupert. The Prince

embraced him, where he had only nodded to the other Englishman who had made low bows to their King's half-Ger-
man nephew.

"My lord of Arundel!" Rupert said. Then he gestured
toward Boye. "My lord, *this* is your gift to me! He is somewhat grown from the day I received him these years past."

Arundel looked at the dog with a serious expression;
then the corner of his mouth twitched. "I believe that I did
after all send you the right gift, Your Highness."

"And I thank you for him! He is an excellent animal."

"So I have been told. The ambassador in Vienna has
written me about you—and about him. The emperor of Austria thinks well of both of you. He admires your prowess
with a boar spear and your dog's courage before a stag."

Arundel would have said more, but a servant in green
velvet livery came up and spoke to the Prince. Rupert
turned back to Arundel, saying, "My uncle awaits me now.
Will I see you again soon?"

Arundel shook his head. "No, Your Highness. I journey
to France and Italy." At the Prince's look of open disappointment, the nobleman went on. "Now, go see the King.
Take my dog with you. Let him be admired." The earl
smiled and turned away.

Boye beside him, Rupert crossed the antechamber.
Doors were flung open for him, and the two strode into the
royal audience chamber. Here, after some ten paces, the
Prince swiftly went down on one knee before the King of
England.

Charles I sat in a chair, not a throne, at the end of a long ribbon of scarlet carpet. In the large stone room, the King seemed small. Charles, compared to Rupert, was a very little man. His face was long and melancholy, his hair, moustache, and goatee a chestnut brown, his eyes also brown in his pale face. He wore a suit of violet satin and his wide black hat bore a white plume.

Henrietta Maria, his tiny French-born Queen, had long dark ringlets, large dark eyes, and a fine complexion. Her gown was of purple satin. Large pearls gleamed about her throat. The Queen of England was not at all beautiful. She was very thin, one shoulder higher than the other, and her teeth protruded. These things, though, were quite forgotten when she spoke. Because Charles was very shy, the Queen greeted the Prince first. Her manner was, as always, lively and charming, her English sweetly accented by her French background. "How you have grown, Rupert! You are very, very large!"

"Aye, very large!" agreed King Charles, who put out his delicate hand to his nephew. "I congratulate you on your release from Austria."

"Thank you, Your Majesty. Thank you for aiding me to procure it."

The Queen spoke again, this time in French. "Is this the dog from Vienna—the dog Arundel sent you?"

"It is, Your Majesty."

"*Mon Dieu,* he is a fine animal—and very large too. Does he like children?"

"My small sister, Sophie, is fond of him. Poodles like children, though Boye has so far been with few."

Henrietta Maria smiled. *"Bien,* our daughter will be pleased with him. She is here, also, at Dover." The Queen nodded toward Boye, then snapped her fingers for him to come to her. At Rupert's push the poodle came to her chair and permitted her to stroke his mane.

Charles was gloomy. "Rupert, my nephew, matters in England are very dangerous these days. Some men say we shall have civil war. I, myself, do not believe this. I do not wish to believe it, for how with a good conscience can a king go to war against his own subjects? My counselors tell me that your presence in England could embarrass me. You have the repute of a fierce soldier. The Parliament will say at once that I have sent for you to lead my armies. I do not choose to permit the Parliament, which is filled with my Roundhead enemies, to inflame the people of my kingdom with this rumor, so I must send you back to the Nether-lands. Three days from now the Queen and the princess sail for The Hague. You will sail with them and escort them to the Stadtholder."

Rupert bowed his head. He could not disobey his uncle and give him further trouble, but the young man was sad-dened by the news.

The King of England spoke again, more jovially this time. "Tonight you shall take supper with us. We shall speak of your mother and your brothers and sisters. Too, we shall hear of your long captivity among the Austrians."

"Rupert," put in the Queen, who seemed more under-standing than Charles, "if it should fall out that we must have war here in England—war between our forces and those of Parliament, be assured of this. We shall at once send for you and for your brother, Maurice. I do not leave England willingly now, myself. I must seek military help from the Dutch if we have civil war here." She smiled at her husband's tall nephew. "Now go. Have someone take you to the princess. She is lonely here, she says. Her brothers are not with her. Take your beautiful white dog to her! Let him entertain her."

Prince Rupert bowed low and left the castle chamber. Once outside, he paused to speak to Boye. "I wish for your sake that the King's oldest lad, Prince Charles, were here. By now he would be nearly twelve years old. A rough frolic he would give you, if I remember him. You will have to behave in a gentle manner toward his sister." Rupert laughed his harsh laugh. "It seems to me we have come to England only to be playfellows to a girl but ten years old. I had not expected this. 'Tis a pity I cannot walk on my hind legs and bark to amuse her, but I have no such talents. If I had brought little Joliffe with me, perhaps he would know how to entertain her.

"Come, Boye, we seek a princess!"

Chapter IV

General of the King's Horse

SPRING AT THE HAGUE was pleasant for Boye. He liked the broad green lawns bordering the canals, and he found chas-ing the Netherlands' white storks safer sport than fighting swans. But as the slow lazy months passed by he became more and more aware of Rupert's and Maurice's growing restlessness. He caught their nervousness himself, and barked and howled as they paced their poor lodgings.

From February through July, the young soldier-princes waited in the Netherlands. Then, early in August, the long-awaited message came at last. Henrietta Maria, the English Queen, sent Rupert a commission as general of the King's Horse, his cavalry. King Charles had departed from London angrily. Once he had left his chief city to the Parliament, he began to call men to him, men who agreed with his views and who also disliked the arrogance of the Parliament. Charles wanted soldiers, experienced soldiers. Although Rupert was only twenty-three years old, the Cavalier army, loyal to Charles I, needed him and Maurice desperately. Few Englishmen had experienced war, for England had known peace for some time. Good officers for either King or Parliament were hard to come by.

Maurice shouted with joy when Rupert showed him the Queen's commission. "It's come—at last!" He caught Boye by the mane. "I'll teach you no more tricks now, my lad. There'll be no time for that."

"You've taught him enough, brother," was Rupert's dry comment. "He frisks about on forepaws and hindquarters, prays, bows, and barks at the moon. He has amused Sophie enough and very much offended the Dutch by his pretended prayers. If you had free rein, my *pudelhund* would be a fit cur for a wandering knave from Italy. Bear in mind, Maurice, that Boye is a soldier's dog—not one of our mother's beasts."

Maurice was suddenly somber as he put in, "Aye, Rupert, now we obey our English uncle. We say farewell, then take our rags of clothing, our swords, and. . . ."

"My dog," interrupted the older prince, "and hie ourselves to England."

The three soon departed aboard a Dutch ship given them by the Stadtholder. The princes brought with them to

England a store of gunpowder, muskets, an engineer, and an expert on the use of gunpowder. Their sails were set for Scarborough, an English port, but on the way they were challenged by Parliament's ships.

As usual Rupert was seasick. He depended on Boye's strength to get around the decks. By holding firmly to Boye he staggered about with Maurice, who was a far better sailor than he.

Nevertheless, the Prince would not go below when the enemy pursued them. "If they board us, the Roundheads will search us. They'll take the muskets and powder we carry for King Charles and use them for their own armies," he told his brother and the Dutch captain. The deck lurched just then. Rupert would have fallen except that Boye braced himself to take much of his master's weight on his shoulder. "There are three Parliament ships—and *one* of us!"

"What shall I do, Your Highness?" asked the frightened Dutchman.

"They must not search this ship!" replied Rupert. "Bring muskets from below decks. If we must, we shall fight."

As Rupert's ship made swift headway under the driving wind, one of the Roundhead vessels fired her cannon to the leeward. The other two parliament ships swiftly followed the first, sailing to the attack.

The poodle stood on the deck, the sea wind fresh on his face as he drank in the excitement, all the rushing to and fro

and the wild shouting. Rupert, his seasickness forgotten, released Boye and made his way to the rail. The dog ran to
him to put his front paws on it, too, as his master fired a
musket at the pursuing ship. Rupert's was only a token shot.
It fell far short of the Roundhead vessels, which were out of
all but cannon range. Yet it greatly pleased both princes.

Maurice clapped Boye on the back as if the dog had
been a man. "How do you like your first taste of war, my
lad? I saw him, Rupert! Your dog did not flinch—not even
when the Roundheads fired their great guns at us."

"Boye is a soldier's dog," was all Rupert said in reply.

Soon the smaller Dutch ship outran the larger, clumsier
English ships, and the captain put the princes and Boye into
a small boat outside the harbor of Tynemouth. He would
later make for Scarborough, but Rupert chose not to. He did
not want to be captured by the Roundheads; Tynemouth
was safer for him and Maurice.

Rupert sat in the stern of the small boat with Boye. The
gray seawater was rough, white capped, and very near
them. Rupert noticed with pleasure that the poodle did not
seem afraid.

Only a few men met the soldier princes at Tynemouth.
They brought orders for them to ride to King Charles.
Horses were much swifter than a coach, so Boye must run
beside his master's horse. Run he did for several miles. But
it was an unusual year, and furthermore, in spite of the fact
that it was still summer the ground was unseasonably icy.

Rupert had some bad luck. He was galloping in the lead with one of his escort when suddenly his mount slipped. It neighed in fright as it slid across a wet spot in the road; then in its panic it reared, throwing Rupert to the ground.

The animal fell but soon scrambled to its feet and stood trembling, obedient to an officer's shouted command. The horse was unharmed; Rupert was not so fortunate. He lay in the road, sprawled out in an unnatural manner on one side.

As he tried to get up and fell back, one of the officers and Maurice dismounted. They hurried to Rupert while Boye, who had ranged ahead, came running back at Maurice's whistle.

"Are you harmed, Your Highness?" cried the officer, kneeling beside the Prince.

"Aye," Rupert groaned, " 'Tis my shoulder!" His face was white with pain.

Boye, frantic at his master's trouble, bounded to Rupert and tried to lick his face.

Maurice called the poodle off. "Let him be, Boye! Down!"

The officer spoke. "We are but a mile from Northallerton. I'll send a man for the bonesetter," and he left to give a trooper the command.

The moment the trooper had galloped away, Boye moved in as close as he could to his master, who lay so still.

"Let him be, Boye!" ordered the younger prince once more.

"Aye, lad, let me be," Rupert also told the dog.

Boye subsided to lie down, his troubled eyes on his master, who groaned when he was forced to move.

The trooper was back far more quickly than expected. With him came a thickset man on a large sorrel horse. He was the village bonesetter, who by good chance had been at home.

"You'll set my brother's shoulder," Maurice told him.

The man looked down at Maurice from his horse. "Perhaps I will. Perhaps I won't. It depends on who ye'd be." His gaze took in the Prince's plain cloak and the plumeless hats of the officers who rode with Maurice and Rupert. Wisely King Charles had not sent out his men in their customary silks, velvets, and satins into northeast England, where they could easily meet Roundhead enemies. Then the bonesetter's gaze fell on Boye. He eyed him for a short time and looked back to Maurice. " 'Tis a fine dog," he told him, "fine enough for a great lord. Who'd ye be? Ye garb yerselves like unto Roundheads, but ye've not cropped yer hair. I'm a King's man. Ye'd best know this before ye trust a Roundhead to my care."

Rupert's laugh was a shaky one. "No Roundheads are we! I am Prince Rupert, new come from the Netherlands. King Charles is my uncle. These gentlemen are with me— loyal Cavaliers every one of them. The dog is mine."

The bonesetter nodded and dismounted. "I'll tend to ye then, if ye be King's men—no matter who ye be." He went toward the Prince and bent over him, opening his shirt to see his shoulder.

When the newcomer approached his master, Boye stiffened; when the man dared touch the Prince, the dog growled. Maurice lunged toward him too late. Boye had already sprung forward and leaped onto the bonesetter, sending him sprawling forward on his face. Then, protecting his master, Boye stood over him, snarling.

"Call off that demon!" shouted the man from Northallerton. "Or find someone else to set the shoulder."

Rupert spoke to the dog above the bonesetter's head. "Boye, go to! Lie down! This man means me no harm! Go, Boye. Go!"

At last, and with misgivings, the poodle stepped some paces away from his master and let the bonesetter do his work. Boye would not lie down, however, and Maurice came to stand beside him and hold his collar.

"Cry out, Your Highness, if it will make ye easier when I put yer shoulder back to joint," the bonesetter told Rupert.

The Prince turned his head with an effort and looked at the poodle. "I think I'd best not groan. Boye would come at you again." Rupert grinned at Maurice. "Brother, can you hold him fast?"

Maurice was grinning, too. "I am not so certain that I can."

Another Cavalier came now to help Maurice, who told his brother, "Keep your silence, Rupert, so the bonesetter can keep his life!"

The bonesetter worked very swiftly once he heard this. Rupert made no sound other than a grunt when his bones were manipulated back into their sockets. Even at that faint sound Maurice and the other Cavalier were hard put to keep the rearing poodle under control. Then, when the bonesetter had finished and stood up, Boye was released. He growled first at the bonesetter before he ran, at Rupert's whistle, to where his master lay and licked his face and hands.

"What shall we pay you for your services?" Rupert asked the man from Northallerton.

"I am usually paid two shillings for my work. Round-head bones I will set for five shillings. From ye, gentlemen of the King, I'll take but one shilling!"

"Give him one shilling," Rupert told his brother. "And I give you my thanks and apologize to you for the conduct of my dog," he said to the bonesetter.

The man took the shilling, nodded, and looked long at Boye before he swung up into his saddle. " 'Tis a demon of a dog ye have there," he told the Prince. "If he attacks Roundheads half so hotly as he attacks loyal folk, he'll soon make a name for himself in England. Ye've come to fight?"

"Aye," Rupert told him.

"I believe ye truly are who ye say ye are—though at

first I misdoubted ye. I believe ye do be Prince Rupert, the one folk name the Devil. If ye were another man, I'd tell ye to get yerself now to bed, but I doubt if ye would, so I'll have a coach sent ye."

Rupert had a smile for the loyal bonesetter. "How soon can I ride? I seek no bed now, and I want no coach."

"In three hours' time, with some good warm wine in ye. There be an inn not far from here—the Unicorn. Make yer way there, gentlemen. Ye'll find the innkeeper a King's man, too, but he'll ask more than one shilling from ye." With these words the bonesetter jogged off homeward in the chilly afternoon.

The Prince stroked Boye's head while he gathered the strength to get up. "You showed the stuff you're made of," he told the dog. "Already they name me Rupert the Devil here in England. Boye, they'll name you the Devil's dog perhaps?"

"If they don't call both of you somewhat worse. Now let us go to the Unicorn," put in Maurice, who took up his brother's shirt while men of the escort picked up his other clothing and sword. Three hours later they were once more on their way.

In three days they arrived in Nottingham and Rupert, whose shoulder pained him badly, was put to bed in an inn. Though Maurice attended the King, Boye remained with his master. It did no good for Rupert to try to send the dog off for exercise with his younger brother. With his master abed,

Boye would not go farther away than the door of the inn chamber.

He was lying on the foot of the Prince's bed when a visitor, the King's appointed governor of Nottingham, came into the room. The man spoke in a breathless manner.

"Your Highness, I have come on an important matter. The King has sent to me from Coventry, where he has recently journeyed, a request for two petards from the arsenal here."

"How does that request from my uncle concern me, my lord?" demanded Rupert.

The governor smiled, looking embarrassed, and spread out his small white hands. "I do not know what a petard is! Neither do any of my officers. Since we knew you were resting here, and are an experienced soldier, we thought. . . ."

"True warriors I find here!" commented Rupert harshly. "I take it you have come to ask me to point out a petard to you? 'Tis a thing which blows up when trod upon!"

The governor's face reddened with anger, but he said, "Yes, Your Highness. That is what I ask of you—to show me a petard."

"Then I suppose I must leave my bed and go to the arsenal with you?" Rupert reached for his shirt, hanging on a chairback near him, put it on, and heaved himself out of bed. He got to his feet and painfully drew on the rest of his clothing. Boye leaped down off the bed and stood steady as Rupert took the dog's collar.

The animal knew his master was weak; he felt how the Prince put a good deal of his weight on him as they left the inn and walked to the arsenal, which luckily for Rupert was not far away. The two men were silent on the way to that building.

Once inside it Rupert strolled slowly about with Boye at his heels. He examined the piles of cannonballs, the stacked muskets, pikes, pistols, swords, and body armor. Finally, with a sigh, he turned to the satin-clad governor and said, "There are no petards here, my lord."

"But the King *demands* petards, Your Highness."

"Then make them! Is there no soldier in Notttingham who has experience of these matters?"

"I know of none." The governor touched his moustache, frowning. "Ah, Major Legge—perhaps?"

"Well, fetch him at once. I shall wait."

The governor sent his serving man to scour about for the major while Rupert sat on a bench, waiting. The Prince whistled idly, patted his dog, and looked about him at the arms and armor but never did he address the fuming governor, who felt himself humiliated.

William Legge, who presently appeared, was a tall man with a long, plain, smallpox-scarred face, brown hair, and sharp brown eyes. His clothing was simple, almost shabby, his smile a warm one. There was an acrid odor about him— that of gunpowder. Boye liked it.

"Major Legge, can you make petards?" asked Rupert.

"I can, Your Highness," said the soldier, who had been told by the governor's manservant whom he was to see.

"Out of what?" demanded the governor so loudly that he startled Boye.

"Out of apothecary's mortars, my lord. They will explode, I assure you, when I construct them!"

Rupert laughed and waved his hand toward the royal governor of Nottingham, dismissing him. "Betake yourself to your other duties, my lord. I'll speak with this *soldier*."

Then the Prince gave his full attention to Legge. "Make two petards! But first, where have you served before, Major Legge?"

"In the service of the king of Sweden and of the Stadtholder of the Netherlands. I came home to England some years ago to serve as a lieutenant of ordnance for the Scottish War." Legge had been looking at Boye. There was a question in his eyes, and after a moment's waiting he asked it. "Your Highness, is this the dog you brought with you from Austria?"

"He is. Greet Major Legge," Rupert ordered the poodle.

Will laughed when Boye gave him his paw. "He's certainly no demon that I can see."

Rupert's words were sober ones, "To us, to you and me and to all men loyal to King Charles, Boye will not seem evil. To the Roundheads I am told he will be the Devil's dog because that is what they name me."

"They call you more than that, Your Highness,—the

Roundheads do," Will Legge told the Prince. "They say you are a wizard come over from the Netherlands!"

"Then perhaps 'tis witch dog you'll be, Boye!" said the Prince to the dog.

When Legge had gone, Rupert spoke to Boye again. "I think we have a friend in the petard maker, and I know I will need him. Aye, lad, I know what I am called—devil, wizard, and even among my own Cavaliers, the German, because my father was a German prince. We shall need good friends like Will Legge, you and I. You must be lonely, Boye, for the company of little Joliffe, eh? I have Maurice, my brother, with me. You have no child and no other dog to keep you company!"

As soon as Rupert's shoulder would permit, he left Nottingham for Coventry with Maurice, Boye, and Will Legge. They did not find the King there as they had expected. Coventry had closed its gates against him, and Charles I had ridden away to more hospitable Leicester. There the Prince caught up with him. Rupert now saw for the first time the odd lot of men out of whom King Charles's cavalry was to be forged.

Boye was told, "Sit" while his master rode up and down the lines of mounted men. The poodle, who disliked this command, found the sidelines distasteful. He did not find the troops his master was to command exciting either. There were no drums and trumpets with them. Soldiers to him meant music and happy shouting—as at The Hague, when the Stadtholder's army paraded and drilled. He still remembered the excitement.

The prince, too, found his troopers an unhappy sight. They were a mangy appearing group. Only a few of the men who had ridden to King Charles were dressed and mounted alike, and they were merely retainers of some particular cavalier lord—not men of military experience. Some few wealthy folk had come to the King's call and brought their sons and servants with them, dressed alike as much as possible. Most of the men, however, had ridden to Leicester alone. They wore what they left home in, and they brought the best horses they could find. The only encouraging thing Rupert could see clearly was that each English cavalryman sat his horse easily and well.

When the Prince came back to Boye, he did not try to conceal his disappointment. Boye heard his sigh; Will Legge listened to his words. "They know not one thing of war, Will. They have never heard the great guns. They have fired the musket only when they hunted deer. I find them ill fed; a number are ill horsed, too. Some of them even have the look of thieves about them."

"That is not strange, Your Highness. You are new come to England," Legge told the Prince. "A few of them were accused by the farmer folk of Leicester of entering hen houses by moonlight. When the thieves were arrested, they were freed by their companions who took them from prisons by force. The men defied their own officers."

"How many cavalrymen does the King have, Will?" the Prince asked.

"Eight to ten troops—perhaps five hundred men. New men come each day to the King."

"How many do our spies say the Roundheads have?" At his master's tone Boye rose to his feet hopefully, expecting to be called, but no, Rupert disappointingly continued speaking to Legge.

"Seventy-five troops of horse, five of dragoons."

The Prince spoke grimly. "It is what I had expected. The Roundheads, the men who are now the Parliament, have money. The money which most easily comes to hand lies in London, and the Roundheads hold London. Too, the King can gather no taxes." Rupert sighed. "Armies are costly."

"Aye, one troop of theirs is so well armored that even the Roundheads call them the Lobsters." Major Legge's laugh was without humor.

"And we lack even muskets, Will! We have no money. We have only our swords." Rupert gazed toward Boye who now stood, still as a stone. "We have courage," he added, "though we do not always obey commands well, it seems. Look there to Boye, for example. I commanded him to sit. He stands. But we have right on our side. King Charles was chosen by God to be king. I pray only that we can meet

Parliament's forces with equal forces. I hope to make cavalry out of this lot of men. It is a hard task, indeed!" The Prince sighed again. "I trust when we win our first battle, the war will end. Then the King can return to London."

Legge was an honest man and did not seek popularity at the expense of truth. "You do not know the temper of these Roundheads, Your Highness, though you know that of our own men well enough. The Roundheads will not rest content if we win the first battle—not even if we win battle after battle. They will come at us again and again."

"Then I, Rupert the Devil, must teach them the folly of their behavior. Come to me, Boye!" Rupert called. The dog bounded forward until he was beside his master's black horse.

Rupert was very splendid this late summer day. His coat, breeches, boots, and hat were ebony black. Over all he wore a new scarlet cloak, a gift of the King, and in his hat was a white plume. About his neck in place of the usual broad collar he wore a scarf of white lace. That morning the harried Prince had cut himself shaving and had knotted the lace about his neck to stop the bleeding.

Not one cavalryman who stared at the young general of the King's Horse was unaware of any detail of his leader's costume. Each in his own mind resolved to copy it. The troopers were equally aware of the great white dog who now stood, his tail wagging because he was being noticed again, beside the Prince.

" 'Tis the dog who brings him luck," one trooper whispered to another. "He's named Rupert's luck, I hear."

"Aye," agreed the second man, who didn't know his error. "The dog is a talisman. I have heard it was he who secured the Prince's wonderful escapes from three Austrian prisons. The dog has marvelous powers! Folk do say he is a witch!"

Chapter V

Battle Dog

BOYE FOUND the next weeks among the most frustrating and boring in his life. The Prince had little time for him. Each day was like every other day. Rupert drilled, drilled, and drilled the troopers while the dog stood or sat and watched. He had his master's attention only in the evenings when the day's drilling was ended. Rupert was determined he would make fine cavalry out of the troopers who had awaited him at Leicester, but it was no easy process and he was doubtful of his success. As he once said to Maurice and to Will, with whom he was now inseparable, "For the most part, as you know too well, my men do not have pistols nor do they possess muskets. Each man has a sword, however. On the sword I must rely. My troopers will use them only. They will not reply to the musket fire of the Roundheads at all.

No, they will sweep down on them at a gallop and put the Roundheads to their swords."

Will had looked thoughtful and reached for his wine cup when he heard these words. "Aye, it is untried, but I think it would take the gangrel Parliament men by surprise."

Maurice laughed. "The old cavalry charge is a ridiculous thing. In Germany troopers charge at a trot and fire a volley at every one hundred sixty yards. By the time they reach the enemy ranks, half of them are dead. From what I have seen of the rabble you command, brother, a swift charge would be the wisest course. Get it over with as soon as possible, I say. They have neither the wit nor the discipline for anything else, and it fits their nature."

"We shall have our first parade on Saturday," Rupert told the others with a smile. He touched Boye with the toe of his boot and the dog rolled over on signal to have his belly scratched, a thing he loved. "Aye, Boye, on that day of all days you will sit at attention beside me while I inspect my troopers. You will be an example of discipline to my men. If a dog can be taught to be a soldier, why not Cavaliers, though I despair of ever convincing you that one does not wag his tail while at attention. Maurice, you were not able to teach him that!"

"Do you think you will be able to keep your *men* on parade?" Maurice wanted to know.

"I trust I can. Then we ride to Nottingham to see the

King set up the royal standard. After that we shall see what we shall see where the Roundheads are concerned."

The poodle greatly enjoyed the noisy parade at Leicester. He sat rigid beside his mounted master as rank after rank of white-sashed Cavaliers trotted by and took Rupert's salute. An old serving man who had temporarily joined the two princes at Leicester had clipped the poodle to Rupert's satisfaction, then washed and brushed him, and finally polished the brass studs on his collar. As the men with thundering kettledrums and loud trumpets first paraded past, Boye wanted to dash forward and walk with them, but at a command from Rupert he sat once more.

The corners of the Prince's mouth twitched with amusement when he overheard what two of the watching townsfolk of Leicester said of him and his dog. During a lull in the music when only the jingling sound of the bridles of the troopers in their ragged lines could be heard, someone behind Rupert too loudly remarked, " 'Tis Rupert the Devil and his witch dog. Them two'll scare the Roundheads."

"Rupert the Robber, 'tis what some folk hereabouts call the Prince." The second speaker was as drunk as the first. "His troopers, curse 'em, steal whatever takes their fancy and nary a farthing of payment do we see. They say his dog can make hisself invisible. 'Tis how we lose the hens from our hen houses. The dog takes 'em—more clever than any fox he is!"

"Go to!" said the first man. "They but take from Roundheads, not from folk loyal to King Charles. Would ye be a Roundhead, yerself, to talk so of the Prince?"

There was the loud smack of a blow.

Boye heard this and in spite of his discipline turned his head to his left. Two men, both swaying with drunkenness, were trying to trade blows but only one in three landed.

"Boye! Eyes front!" came Rupert's curt order, and the poodle obeyed, looking at the troopers again through the stinging cloud of brown dust the hooves of their horses sent his way.

Three days later Rupert and Maurice rode to Nottingham to be present on the twenty-second of August when King Charles set up the royal standard. This was the King's signal to all Englishmen that he was truly bent on civil war. Boye hated this ceremony as much as he had liked the Leicester parade. The twenty-second was a wretchedly cold and wet day. The King's standard was raised on a hill in pouring rain. This was an ill omen, an officer who stood near the King muttered to another Cavalier, whose fine velvet coat was soaked through. Rupert heard the remark and shot the man a hard glance, which silenced him. The Prince and Boye were as miserably wet as anyone else; Rupert saw how the sodden dog shivered in the cold wind. Yet the poodle stayed at attention as a soldier's dog should. Rupert's frequent glances at Boye were proud ones.

As soon as they were back before a warm hearth in their Nottingham inn, Rupert toweled Boye and sent for a bowl of hot milk, bread, and honey. "It will not do for you to take an ague now. The King sends us back at once to Leicester to continue training his cavalry."

While the dog ate, Maurice entered and dropped his wet cloak onto the floor. "The King goes, himself, to Shrewsbury," he told Rupert. "Then it is said he will ride south toward Oxford and Worcester." He went to the fire and stood with his back to it. "The Earl of Essex, the Roundhead general, will oppose us, it seems. Essex has had some experience of war; he is more than twice your age, Rupert."

"And what of that?" exclaimed the Prince. "Boye, here, knows more of war than the rabble Essex leads. I do not expect this war of our uncle's to be of any great moment as wars go—not half so important as the wars we have seen in Germany. I think I shall soon join the King with my troopers."

But the Prince did not. Boye was well aware of his master's growing depression in the three weeks that followed their return to Leicester. Rupert and his cavalry were not sent for. Also the war went very badly for the King's forces. Will Legge had been taken prisoner by the Roundheads in a skirmish the day after King Charles had erected his standard at Nottingham. Rupert and Maurice missed Will. So did the poodle. Will was a good-natured man who delighted in dogs and who had kept Boye with him as much as possible when Rupert was occupied with his everlasting drilling. Now sometimes while Rupert looked on, approving and disapproving, as his junior officers shouted at the per' spiring, wheeling troopers, Boye sought the September sun' shine and slept the dull day away. He was eager to romp at night but found his master always too tired, so the dog padded restlessly and silently about their inn lodgings until near dawn, while Rupert slept.

The other news that came to the cavalrymen at Lei' cester was also evil, though it did not concern Boye as did the loss of Will Legge. One of the King's officers had early in the month surrendered Portsmouth to the Roundheads. Other important harbors, too, were now in Roundhead hands —Hull, Bristol, and Plymouth. With these held by the enemy, how was the King to receive supplies from Europe? The King's navy had deserted to the enemy, and so Round' heads ruled the seas.

Two days after Portsmouth was surrendered the Earl of Essex marched west with his army from London to catch and attack the King at Worcester. This was not good news either, nor was the message which came to Rupert that Ox' ford had been abandoned to the enemy. Oxford had ever been a city loyal to the King. Now Roundhead soldiers de' stroyed its churches and cathedral, smashed furniture and slashed pictures in the homes of Cavalier families. At Ox' ford the Roundheads passed their time throwing rocks through the valuable stained-glass windows of the various colleges and shooting their muskets and pistols at the stone statues on the buildings.

After the abandonment of Oxford a courier came from the King to Rupert—bringing news that made the Prince get up from his chair at supper. At his shout Boye leaped to his feet from where he lay dozing before the hearth. "We are to ride to Worcester, Maurice! The King asks for a strong body of Horse!" he exclaimed. "The Cavalier commander of the Oxford garrison, when he retreated before the Roundheads came, took a chest of treasure to Worcester. I am to look after him and that chest!" Rupert crumpled the paper the courier had brought and threw it into the hearth flames. "At last! Perhaps now we can come to grips with the Roundheads if Essex takes his army toward Worcester!"

Boye found Worcester an interesting place. He liked the nearby rivers, the Severn and the Teme, because sometimes Rupert or Maurice would take him hunting there for waterfowl. He had not been able to retrieve for a huntsman for months. What a joy it was for him to leave camp life and throw himself with a magnificent splash into the water to bring back a teal to his master! The poodle also enjoyed the city walls. At one time Worcester had been a fortified town with strong walls, but now in some places they had fallen into a gray jumble of decayed stone. A high springing dog could often reach the top of a crumbling place and from there leap higher yet to walk upon the wall itself, and gaze down into the old city or, sniffing the hay-scented air, look out onto the countryside of orchards and fields.

Wisely, Rupert had decided that Worcester's ancient walls could not be defended against the enemy. He sent the treasure chest and the men who accompanied it to the north to catch up with the King, who had left Worcester.

The Prince planned to follow soon after, but as he told Maurice one evening at the Star Inn, "The scouts I have sent out tell me that Roundheads have been spied not far from here. Before we abandon Worcester to their mercies, I think I'll take some troops out and have a look at the countryside on the morn. Boye comes. Yes, Boye comes!" The dog had put a paw on his master's knee, and Rupert now spoke directly to him as if Boye had asked him a question.

Rupert laughed and stroked the poodle's head. "Aye, you know those words, lad. That is what I said. I do not conceive of any great peril tomorrow." The young man laughed harshly. "I should like at least one sight of the enemy!"

So the next morning Rupert, Maurice, and several other officers rode out of Worcester with two hundred fifty of the Prince's troopers behind them. Beside Rupert's horse loped Boye, pleased as always with the prospect of a run in the country. Now and again Rupert spoke to him or called him back when he went far to the left or the right of the cavalry to course after a hare that had crossed their path.

The morning jaunt Boye found a pleasant one. The aft-

ernoon, though, grew unusually hot for late September, and
the dog panted as he ran along. Although the troopers were
not encumbered by leather or metal body armor, the Prince
finally called a halt because of the heat. Rupert and his
fellow officers dismounted. They lay down on a hilltop in
the tall, cool grass beneath elm trees. The Prince sat against
a tree, opened his shirt, and fanned himself with his hat.
Attracted by the playful movement of the hat, Boye
bounded toward him and bowled him over. For a few minutes his master played roughly and teasingly with the dog,
but it was hard work for the Prince to roll the big white
animal about and pin him down. The officers and troopers
watched, chuckling at the Prince's efforts, until Rupert, hot
and winded, gave up, laughed—a sound the troopers seldom
heard—and fell back on the grass, exhausted.

Maurice called out, "Boye's too strong for you Rupert?
You'll have no ease with him. It is too warm to wrestle. Send
him off to nose out a brace of hares for our supper."

"Aye, hare pie would suit me well enough." Rupert got
up now, brushed leaves, twigs, dirt, and dog hairs from his
coat. Boye stood before him, eager for the next mock combat, but his master was not about to grant his hope. "Go,
Boye," Rupert commanded him. "Find a hare!"

The dog was disappointed, but knew better than to try
to play with the Prince again. Rupert's mood had changed.
Boye turned about and started slowly away from the Cavaliers. He had understood the command. First, though, he

wanted to drink. Then he would chase hares. His nose told him there was water not far off.

He did not hear Maurice's words as he ambled off down toward the brook below the hilltop. "I'll wager there's not a cursed Roundhead between here and London. Where the devil are they?"

The jumble of jesting answers and comments to Maurice's question did not concern Boye. He crossed the field below and went out onto the road, standing there for a moment gazing toward Powick Bridge, which crossed the stream. Then he went on to the brook and thirstily drank from it.

As he drank, a sound came to his ears. The dog lifted his muzzle from the water and pricked his ears forward. He heard the sound of the hooves of horses, slowly moving horses, and then he caught the rumble of men's voices. Was that his master calling him? Or was it Maurice? Were they mounting up on the hilltop and leaving him? Boye continued to listen. No, he did not know those voices. He sniffed the air, but no scent came to him. The wind was wrong. Again the frightening idea came to Boye that his master was riding away, leaving him, a thing the dog dreaded. Boye wheeled about now and dashed up onto the bank.

There he discovered the source of the sounds. They came from over the little bridge—not from Rupert's direction at all. As the dog crouched by the roadside, he saw a file of mounted men come riding slowly out of a wooded lane toward him. These men wore coats of buff-colored leather. Their helmets were of steel. He had their scent now. Whoever these men were, they were strangers to him. Wary, Boye avoided being seen by them. In one great leap, the poodle, a white streak, was over the road. At a rush he crossed the field and still at a run came crashing up the hill to where his master took his ease.

Rupert's brother saw him first. "What?" he said. "He's back so soon! He's brought us no fat hare for supper." Maurice yawned.

Boye lunged toward Rupert, then barked sharply once. The dog would not come to the Prince's snapped fingers. Instead, he barked again, backed away, turned and trotted toward the rim of the hill.

"What ails the beast?" growled an irritated officer, who'd been awakened by the poodle's bark.

Rupert was on his feet now. "I do not know, but somewhat annoys him. Perhaps 'tis a fat stag he's found for our supper. And we've got no muskets with us!"

Boye barked a third time. He ran forward, looking over his shoulder at his master to make sure he followed. At the lip of the hill man and dog stopped.

There on the field below them they were—a great body of troopers, Roundheads who suspected nothing. Certainly they did not know that two hundred fifty Cavaliers lay on the grass above them.

Boye heard Rupert's gasp of surprise. He felt his master's hand grip his back hard and heard his whisper of pleasure. "Good lad, Boye!" said the Prince. "You are a better scout than any in the King's forces. I believe you meant to show me these strangers, just the ones I sought. Come, Boye, we'll give the alarm!"

At a run, as silent a run as he could manage, Rupert came back to his men. Maurice was still awake and got to his feet when he saw his brother coming. Rupert spoke quietly to him. "The Roundheads deploy in the field below. Arouse the officers. They are to command the troopers to mount and draw their swords—but to do all as quietly as possible. Make haste, I will take the enemy if I can!"

The sunset-lighted hilltop was within minutes a scene of great, but silent confusion. Troopers sprang up everywhere as their officers bent over them, shaking them awake. Then they hurried to their horses. The officers motioned to their men to form up, and their mounts, sensing their riders' excitement, reared when their reins were snatched as the troopers mounted. In the middle of all, Boye kept close by Rupert's horse as he expertly dodged hooves. In moments the Cavaliers were ready.

Rupert then stood up in his stirrups. Without a word he gestured with his sword toward the enemy. Then he gave his black his head. With Boye at the horse's heels, the young general of the King's Horse swept forward down the hill, his troopers thundering after him. Once over its rim the Cava-

liers behind the Prince yelled their defiance to the Roundheads. This fierce sound was one of great delight to the
poodle. He joined it with his deepest full-throated bay as he
ran at top speed.

The Roundheads were caught totally by surprise as the
bright-coated King's troopers came at a gallop, slashing into
them. They were forced back onto the road. Many of them,
howling with terror, fled back across the bridge. Too many
Roundheads at one time attempted to cross the narrow
span. They jammed up together in a melee of cursing men
and struggling mounts.

Boye paid no heed to what went on at the bridge. He
had almost immediately lost his master! The Prince had
crossed the bridge in the first crush of troopers. His dog had
been shouldered aside by a Cavalier's horse and thrown into
the middle of the stream. The bridge was a low one, so Boye
was not hurt. Swimming to the bank and leaping out, he
came, dripping wet, back up onto the road. He waited only
long enough to shake himself, then joined another Cavalier,
a young officer who in an instant's pause in the hand-to-
hand fighting had seen him and called out to him, "Come,
Boye!"

At the side of this trooper's horse, Boye dashed across
the field in pursuit of fleeing Roundheads, who sought only
to escape Rupert the Devil and his cavalrymen. One of the
running Roundheads, a long-nosed man with lank flaxen
hair, had been unhorsed, and he now lunged for the stream.

Boye leaped for him and caught him by the wrist. The trooper went down under the dog's charge, but the man was very strong and on his feet almost at once, throwing off the dog. "Devil's whelp!" he screeched, aiming his cocked pistol at Boye, who crouched for the second attack.

Though his scalp bled badly from a Roundhead sword slash, Maurice, who had seen Rupert thunder across the bridge, had been on the lookout for the poodle. Now he spied him and spurred his mount forward, shouting, "Boye, Boye! Down!" He had seen the Roundhead, whose wrist dripped blood, turn and aim his pistol at the dog. The Prince rode toward him, his sword upraised to cut the man down.

The Roundhead saw his danger now. It came not from the white dog, but from Maurice. He changed his aim and hastily fired at the oncoming horseman, and missed. With a shout of anger the Roundhead threw his useless weapon at the Prince, then flung himself into the stream and began to swim across.

In his excitement Boye would have followed after him to drag him out, but Maurice again called to him. "No, Boye! Come, Boye! Stay with me! Let the Roundhead drown!"

The white dog, confused, followed his commands, though his instincts told him to go into the stream after the enemy he had attacked. With Maurice and other Cavaliers Boye scoured the field pushing the armored Roundheads into the river or slashing them down as they sought to fight their way through the knots of King's men. To the dog this was a wondrous madness of hooves, shouts, ear-splitting cries, and dashing confusion. Boye did not know it, of course, but the battle had truly been won by Rupert's men the moment they had made their surprise charge down the hillside. Most of the Roundheads had galloped away to safety while the poodle was swimming the stream and splashing ashore. Others had fled into the deep brook or been pushed into it over Powick Bridge and, because of their clumsy half armor, had sunk and drowned.

When Rupert returned from his headlong charge, he found the battle ended and the victory his. Boye was first to dash forward to meet him. Rupert immediately made a tour of the field where they had surprised the Roundheads. Forty-five enemy troopers lay dead on the grass. Few Cavaliers had even been wounded. The same laughing young officer who had rescued Boye during the battle brought the Prince the captured Roundhead colors. Another officer escorted the two Roundhead commanders to him. One of them was badly wounded; Rupert sent him immediately to Worcester to a physician. The other man, who would be held prisoner, interested the Prince greatly, for he was a member of Parliament and a particularly important enemy of King Charles. Finally Rupert spoke with Maurice, who sat beside the bridge having his head bandaged with his white Cavalier scarf. "How do you fare, brother?" he asked.

"I think I shall live to win another victory such as this." Maurice gave Rupert a merry grin and reached out from where he sat to touch Boye, who was still damp from his ducking. "Our dog acquitted himself very well. He brought down a Roundhead and gave him somewhat to remember us by, but the man got away into the stream after he tried to shoot me." Maurice laughed. "I would not permit Boye to retrieve such scum."

Rupert was very pleased. "Aye, a soldier's dog he is, it seems," he told his brother. His gaze at Maurice and then at Boye was a loving one. "But I would not have him always a battle dog. He should have been tethered; there was not time. Tethered he shall be, or with the baggage carts from now on!"

"Then find a strong man who can tether him. All England's clack soon will be of Rupert the Devil and of his white dog. Come what may, Boye made his mark this day at Powick Bridge! The Roundheads saw him. They will not forget him. One Roundhead, in particular, will remember him—if he did not drown—the trooper he brought down!" Maurice pulled Boye close. "Aye, lad, you did well today by King Charles. So, Boye, you will not join a second troopers' charge? What does that matter? You have left the print of your teeth in one Roundhead, one who would surely kill you if he could."

Maurice had spoken truly. Safe, three miles away, the

Roundhead trooper, Elnathan Parmenter, sat on a stump binding his bitten wrist with a strip of linen from his shirt. Parmenter was seacoast bred, a strong swimmer. He would not drown, not even with the weight of a leather jerkin and steel helmet.

Parmenter tied the bandage with the help of his teeth and his unwounded hand. Then he got up and began to walk through the plum orchard that sheltered him. He had but two thoughts. The first was to find the army of the Earl of Essex, the main Roundhead army. The second was of vengeance. Elnathan Parmenter was not a man to forget a hurt done him. He told himself this as he walked along while night fell and a pale half moon came into the sky. He had always hated the King, but now his hatred and thoughts of revenge were more fierce and more personal. Spies from Leicester had brought the armies of Parliament rumors of the white dog that accompanied Rupert the Robber everywhere he went. The spies had spoken of the dog as a witch. Parmenter told himself that the dog he'd seen was no ghost animal but very much a flesh-and-blood dog and a vicious one. Now the Roundhead trooper hated the dog first, Rupert second, and King Charles last of all.

"As the Lord is my witness, I will kill that witch dog who has maimed my sword arm!" he said to the unheeding dark woods on either side of him.

With his master, Boye fell back to Worcester, and there

the Cavaliers celebrated the victory of Powick Bridge. Much attention was paid to the poodle who had fought beside the troopers. At a boisterous dinner at the Star Inn, Rupert, who for once drank much wine, banged his tankard on the table and shouted, "Silence!" Then he stood up and spoke. "The flag we took today from the Roundheads travels to the King at Shrewsbury, but my dog does not go to war again! He lacks discipline, it seems. So do you!" The trooper officers roared him down now, but his voice rose above theirs. "Soon we join the King at Shrewsbury. We shall leave Worcester to the Roundheads. Let them defend its rotten walls. I think, though, that we shall taste victory again."

Rupert whistled once, and Boye jumped up onto the table, scattering cups. The Prince called for more wine, and when it was brought to him by the potboy, he lifted his cup high. "I drink to Boye and to our victory!"

"Aye, to victory and to Boye!" shouted Maurice, whose wounded head had not kept him from attending. "Chair him! Chair him! Chair the soldier's dog!" He bellowed.

"To Boye. Chair him!" shouted the other officers, draining their cups as Rupert ordered Boye to sit in a chair at the table where the other heroes of Powick Bridge sat. There, like a man, the poodle spent the riotous evening, being toasted again and again.

As Maurice and the others had prophesied, wondrous tales soon began to circulate in England about the Devil

Prince and his witch dog. Men and women whispered that Rupert, accompanied by a dog who became invisible at will, roamed the countryside in disguise.

One countrywoman, an old widow near Worcester, swore she had seen the Prince, alone and dressed in a humble farmer's smock, enter her land. Because he had said he was hungry, she had fed him.

"Where is your son?" he had asked her.

Unaware of who her caller was, she had replied, "Gone to Worcester to see what those rude knaves, the Cavaliers, do!"

"And what think ye of Prince Rupert?" the stranger had asked her.

"A devil!" the woman answered. "May a plague choke him. Whatever foreign land the Prince came from, I pray that he return. Three times worse off is England since he came to it."

"Aye," her dark-browed visitor had agreed. "I am of the same opinion."

For the food he had eaten, he gave her three shillings. Amazed at the large sum, the country wife had secretly followed him to the end of her land. Who could this stranger be? she asked herself. Later she swore that when she saw him leave her land and cut across a neighbor's field, he had a dog with him, a large white beast with a mane of curling hair!

Other folk had other tales to tell of Rupert and the

poodle. One of the most popular was of the Prince's secret visit to the Earl of Essex's army.

Once more in a countryman's disguise, Rupert, on a gray plow horse, rode leisurely toward Essex's forces. Along the road he met a man who drove a cart filled with apples.

"Where do ye go?" asked Rupert in an altered voice.

"To sell my apples to the Earl of Essex's soldiers."

"Why not sell them to Prince Rupert's men," asked the countryman. "The Roundheads will cheat ye. Cavaliers pay double!"

The apple seller spat over the wheel of his cart. "Cavaliers!" He cursed. "There's a lunatick prince among them. They all be loonies. There's not a penny to be got out of that Devil's men!"

Rupert had laughed to hear this. "I have ten shillings. Will ye sell the apples ye have to me then."

"Aye, that I will—for ten shillings."

"For another shilling, exchange yer clothes with me. Keep my horse for me. I'll borrow yer horse and cart and sell yer apples to the Roundheads. I'll return horse and cart to ye here. Rest easy on that matter."

"Why should ye wear my coat and sell my apples?" the apple seller demanded suspiciously.

" 'Tis a conceit I have—a humor. I have never sold apples before. I think I can sell anything. Come now, take the ten shillings. When I return, I'll give ye another one, a Roundhead shilling."

The apple seller agreed. This countryman seemed

strange but not exactly "lunatick." He exchanged his old steeple hat and coat for Rupert's smock and stood in the road watching the stranger drive off on the seat of his cart.

The Prince was a very successful hawker of apples, but he sought far more than Roundhead farthings and groats, as they later guessed. What better way to count their strength, the numbers of dragoons, musketeers, and pikemen than to ride among them? Rupert was gone for some hours but at last returned to where he'd left the apple seller, who drowsed some feet from the road. The Prince shook him awake to retrieve his smock and to give him his other shilling.

"Ye've sold the apples?" asked the cart owner.

"Aye, every last one of them, and may each have a worm in it!"

Still half asleep, the apple vendor rubbed his eyes. His cart was undamaged, his old horse not even winded, but where, he asked himself, did that great white dog come from, the animal that sat now on the seat? "Where did ye find the dog?" the man asked.

"There is no dog. Rub your eyes again," Rupert told him. And as the man did, the dog vanished.

This was the tale the apple seller later told to Essex's men, who crowded around him to hear. The carter added, " 'Tis all God's truth, I say to you. It was Rupert the Devil, himself! He told me this when he gave me my shilling. He asked me to come to ye and ask your officers how they liked the apples he sold them yesterday. Yes, I saw that dog, Rupert's witch beast, on the seat of this very cart." The man patted the spot and went on, "On this very seat. His eyes gleamed at me like fire coals. With my own eyes I saw him disappear in a puff of smoke when his master whistled to him."

Elnathan Parmenter listened carefully to the apple seller's tale. Even he had bought an apple the day before from the dark stranger in the steeple hat. He had not recog-nized him, though he had had one glimpse of the Prince at Powick Bridge. Parmenter turned away in a rage. "Rupert, Rupert. He *dared* come here to Essex's camp, and he brought that cur with him. Vanished, did he? Who'd believe that but this country fool? The dog was in the cart all the time—so near me, so near. And I did not know. Damme, I missed my chance to kill him. It will come again, I say!"

Chapter **VI**

Edgehill

BY MID-OCTOBER the Prince had deserted Worcester to
Essex's Roundheads, men who promptly disfigured Worcester Cathedral. Reports of their vandalism came to Rupert
as he sat one night with Maurice beside a campfire, Boye's
head on his knee as his master smoked his pipe. "The
knaves," exclaimed the older prince, "the church is an
ancient one! Old King John has lain entombed there for over
four hundred years. Will the Roundheads tip him out of
his tomb?"

"King Charles soon marches to London now that Essex
has left it undefended," remarked Maurice. "Do we cover
his advance, brother?"

"Aye, Maurice, I think we shall. It is a clever thing, our
going to London. There are loyal folks there who secretly

hope for this. They will welcome us. I've believed for some time, as you have often heard me say, it is to London we should march to end this war. That is where we'll catch the leaders of this vile rebellion. I know how to deal with them."

"Do you think the King will give battle to Essex before we go to London, Rupert?"

The older prince stroked Boye's ears, then playfully blew a puff of smoke into the dog's face. Boye sneezed. "I pray we do—though the King much mislikes the killing of his subjects. I pray we have the luck we had at Powick Bridge."

Maurice laughed. His eyes were on the poodle, who lay limp and contented. He reached out and tugged gently at the dog's tail. Boye looked reproachfully at him out of the corner of one eye, but did not move. Said Maurice, "The troopers would tell you, brother, that we have our 'luck' with us."

"Well, my lad," Rupert addressed the dog, "give us a second Powick Bridge—if it pleases you."

Toward the end of that month to Boye's delight and that of both Rupert and Maurice, Will Legge suddenly returned. He rode up to the Prince's campfire early one morning, dismounted, and was greeted first by a wildly leaping poodle. Will embraced the dog, then grasped the hands of the two brothers.

"The Roundheads could not hold me!" the major exclaimed. "Like a fool I rode among them, thinking because they also wore green coats as my men did that they were under my command. I escaped them and made my way to Oxford and joined the King. I bring you a message, Your Highness. The King has started his march to London. You are to cover his advance. Scout for him. Our spies have confirmed that Essex is also on the march out of Worcester, not many leagues behind the King—trying to put himself between London and the Royal Army."

Rupert spoke to Maurice. "We shall send out scouting parties immediately to see if we can spy out the Round-heads. Have the scoutmaster come to me now."

As Maurice left, Rupert flung his arm around Will Legge's shoulders. " 'Tis good to see you again, Will. We had begun to despair of you."

Boye, jealous, was at Rupert's side at once when he saw this gesture of affection. Rupert noticed how the dog be-haved.

"Did you hear of Boye's conduct at Powick Bridge?" he asked Legge.

"Aye, 'tis the talk of the King's army. 'Twas the first thing I heard when I got to Oxford."

A few nights later one of the scouting parties Rupert had sent out came hastily back to his camp. With them they brought two prisoners, sour-faced Roundhead cavalrymen, who sat their horses with their arms tied behind them. They were brought into Rupert's tent, and there he questioned them by lantern light.

Boye lay beside his master's chair. He did not growl at the enemy troopers, but his eyes did not leave them for a moment. Many times they glanced at him. One of them, when the dog once got up, stepped aside very quickly to put himself farther out of Boye's way. The Prince saw the man do this and nodded his head. Here was the trooper who would tell him what he wanted to know.

"You skirmished with my men near the village of Kineton," said Rupert to him, "and you were taken prisoner?"

"Aye," answered the Roundhead, whose face was white as dough as he stood before the terrifying Prince.

"Where is my Lord of Essex's main force?"

"At Worcester still," replied the Roundhead.

"That is a lie. *Where* is Essex?"

The Roundhead trembled. "I do not know."

"That, too, is a lie." Rupert prodded Boye with the toe of his boot. "Rouse yourself, Boye. Shall *you* ask this knave what I choose to know? Boye, go to him!"

Boye got up, stretched, and yawned. Slowly he approached the Roundhead, who backed away in terror, then bellowed, "Call off yer dog, Your Highness. I'll tell ye what ye ask. Essex lies at Kineton this very night!"

Rupert whistled. "Not four miles from where I sit! Who would have guessed it?" He called to his aide across the tent. "The King lies at Edgcott. Send a message to him telling him we understand the enemy is at Kineton. Tell him, too, that I come in person tonight and now send out scouts to assure this news is true. I must convince the King to stand and fight."

The aide dashed outside to give the several orders while the Prince told another Cavalier to secure the prisoners well. When they had been taken out, Rupert arose and put on his cloak. "You will stay here until I return," he said to Boye, going out.

Boye had understood. He was to stay behind. He padded softly to the tent flap and peered out into the night. He would have gone farther, following Rupert, but a sentry, a very young Cavalier trooper, who had heard the Prince's words, barred his way.

"Ye heard his command, dog, did ye not?" said the trooper softly. "I'll not permit ye to go after him."

Disappointed, Boye backed into the empty tent again. He crossed it to the opposite side and there started to dig with his paws. He managed to disarrange the carpet Rupert had put down on the ground to keep out the autumn cold, but try as he might the dog did not make more than a few scratches on the frost-hardened soil. Finally he gave up and sitting alone sent up howl after wretched howl until Maurice came to try to comfort him.

Rupert told King Charles he thought it would be wise to stand and fight while the enemy was so near. He advised his uncle to take his army to a piece of high ground nearby, a place called Edgehill, and there turn about to face Kineton and watch the roads that led south, the roads Essex's Roundheads would travel. Charles heard his soldier nephew out, but would not then give his promise. The King was a stubborn man.

It was an angry Prince who rode back to his own camp and who with Boye, Maurice, and Will tramped up and down till nearly dawn, cursing the King's stupid older advisers. No one in Rupert's camp closed his eyes that night—not with the Roundheads so near. The troopers shivered in their blankets beside cold campfires, fires that had been extinguished the moment Rupert had given out the intelligence learned from the Roundhead prisoner.

At four o'clock in the morning a courier galloped in from the King with a letter for Rupert. The Prince called for a lantern, read the message, and then broke into a bay of joy. "We ride to Edgehill where we wait for Essex. 'Tis Sunday and a blessed day I think 'twill be for us!"

Rupert's Cavaliers moved out at once for Edgehill some five miles southeast of Kineton. He and his men alone occupied the top of the hill, their faces turned to the windy north, their eyes straining across the open country for the first view of the enemy. All that morning they waited for Essex to come and for King Charles's troops to arrive.

Boye stood, the cold breezes of late October ruffling his white mane. He was at his usual place at the stirrup of Rupert's horse. The quiet excitement of the men about him was contagious. He longed to bark and dash about as they longed to shout and charge, but he gave way to his desires no more than they—though the men were hard put to keep their places on the hill when they first saw the glint of the morning sun on the helmets of Essex's men below them to the north. The Roundheads, on their part, at once marked out the black line of horsemen against the sky, and they halted, waiting too, for reinforcements.

At one o'clock in the afternoon, to Rupert's relief, King Charles and his army straggled in to join the Prince's cavalry. Charles, who had arrived by a coach, now moved swiftly. He placed his cannon atop the hill, got his foot soldiers into line, and deployed his cavalry to augment Rupert's. Then the King took a horse and rode up to speak to his nephew. With him came a body of officers and two boys on dapple-gray horses, his sons, Prince Charles and Prince James.

While the King and Rupert conferred, the lads looked down at the Prince's white dog. Though they had heard much of him, it was the first time either of them had seen him. " 'Tis our cousin's dog. 'Tis the dog the Roundheads call the witch dog and our father's men Rupert's luck," exclaimed the older boy, thirteen-year-old Charles, the Prince of Wales, to nine-year-old James, Duke of York.

James was enchanted with Boye. "Aye, he is a fine dog. I wish he were mine," James said loudly, loudly enough for Rupert to overhear them.

The Prince called out, "Come, Boye, come!" Then, the dog walking beside his horse, Rupert rode over to his two young cousins. "James, today he *is* your dog! You and your brother shall look after him from a safe place. At Powick Bridge he proved himself so well that he need not show his courage here. Tie him to a tree. I do not want him with me now." The Prince took a leather rope from his coat pocket and gave it to little James. "Have one of your gentlemen secure him well."

The poodle knew that rope and loathed it. He set up a fierce barking and backed away, making the boys laugh, but at Rupert's command he let it be tied to his heavy collar. "Go, Boye! Go with the lads!" Unhappily Boye, at the end of his rope, left with the young princes' stout-armed gentleman leading him. No amount of pulling back and dragging his feet availed the dog. The gentleman was even more deter-mined than he was.

Young Charles and James, their guards and gentlemen rode to the very top of Edgehill, the safest place of all, in Rupert's estimation. There they dismounted and secured their horses to trees. Boye, too, was tied fast and howled his displeasure to the skies.

"The dog wants to join the battle, Charles!" said dark-eyed little James, who had come to stand beside the poodle and try to comfort him.

Charles was plumpish, as swarthy as Rupert, and black-haired as well. "Who does not, James?" sighed Charles. "I do." The older boy had a spyglass with him. He put it to his eye and swept his gaze over the hill and the open plain below. "Why doesn't the battle begin?" he asked one of his gentlemen.

"We believe Lord Essex waits for reinforcements, Your Highness," one man explained to Charles. "We also hope that many Roundheads will desert to us now. We wish to give them time to do so."

Prince Charles snorted. "I doubt this, my lord." He looked over his shoulder at his brother, who sat on the frost-rimed grass next to the poodle. "I'll watch the battle—if there is a battle—through my spyglass, James, and tell you of it."

Boye was suffering a cautious but admiring James to pat him. The lad's words of reply to his older brother meant little to the dog. "Aye, Charles, tell me. I'll understand, and then I'll explain it all to our cousin's dog."

The boys' talk was drowned out by the roar of cannon. A Roundhead gunner had marked out where King Charles stood and fired upon him. The ball fell far short, but the first shot of the battle of Edgehill had been fired. Cavalier cannon replied; more Roundhead cannon answered them.

"What do you see, Charles?" demanded James.

"Rupert! I see our cousin! He rides along the ranks in his scarlet cloak. He's giving directions to the troopers!"

James leaped to his feet and ran to his brother. "Then they'll charge? Now what do you see, Charles?"

"I see the enemy. They face our father. Many of them

wear orange-tawny scarves, the color of Lord Essex's family. Our army moves forward. Down the hill. The tawny scarves move forward, too! Ah, there is the call! Hear it! Hear it, James!"

All who stood at the crest of the hill heard it clearly, the high note of the trumpet that bade Rupert's cavalry charge.

Boye recognized it at once. He had often enough heard that signal when Rupert had drilled his troopers at Leicester. To him it meant but one thing—to run. The dog lunged forward at his rope, trying to break free, but the leather held. Alone, neglected, he plunged to its end again and again, but could not free himself.

The young princes paid no attention to him now. Charles, with his glass still to his eye, shouted to their gentlemen, "We charge the Roundheads. Essex's cavalry sweeps forward to meet our men. No, no!" His voice rose to a high squeal. "I see them! Essex's orange-tawny scarves fire their pistols into the ground—not at our troopers! Rupert's passed through them at a gallop. The tawny scarves turn about. They follow *Rupert!* They've joined *us!*" Charles hugged James. "The tawny scarves were loyal to our father."

"What does Prince Rupert do, Your Highness?" asked the gentleman who had tied the Prince's dog to the tree.

"He rides! He rides like the whirlwind to the north. The Roundhead cavalry flee before him! They'll soon be out of sight. I think they ride to Kineton."

"What of the field below? What of the King and the

foot soldiers? Please, Your Highness, may I have the spy-glass?" asked an old man who stood with the princes. "Rupert will not return, I suspect. There will be no second charge. Kineton is five miles distant. It will take much time for him to regather his wild troopers." The old man sounded disapproving.

Prince Charles surrendered his spyglass and the old man looked through it, muttering. "Too little discipline. Too little training! That is the truth of the matter. Rupert has left the King's foot soldiers unguarded. The other Cavalier horse have also ridden off the field." The man cursed under his breath. "Damme, the enemy infantry has come up to ours. They use musket and pikes against us."

"Do our foot soldiers hold their own?" demanded Charles.

"Aye, Your Highness, we do, though Roundhead cavalry, cavalry that hid itself behind the hedgerows from Rupert, charges down on them now." The old man groaned and waited a long moment, then went on more happily. "They sliced through our ranks, but our men re-form and fight again. They are grouped about the King. I see the King's standard clearly." The old gentleman put down the spyglass and wiped his eyes with his coat sleeves. "My eyes fail me, Your Highness, but I think I mark out Lord Essex, too. Look you among the Roundhead pikemen."

Charles peered eagerly down at the battlefield. "Aye, I do see him and his standard-bearer. Essex wears a tawny scarf and a silvered breastplate. He has a pike in his hand and he leads his men against my father's." Suddenly Charles gave the glass to another gentleman. "I do not think I care to see more. Watch for me."

A now saddened Charles took little James by the arm and led him to where the poodle lay, panting, exhausted by his struggle to pull free. "There's naught to worry *you*," Charles told Boye. "Your master's safe and halfway to Kineton now, but what of our father? What if he's taken prisoner by the Roundheads. And we'd hoped for a quick victory!"

Both boys sat down beneath the leafless tree beside the white dog and pulled their cloaks close about them against the chill wind. As their gentlemen stood outlined against the sky watching and discussing the battle raging below, a dour Charles played with pebbles. James, with tears running down his cheeks, huddled close to him and stroked an equally heartbroken Boye.

Throughout the long afternoon they waited. At sunset the old gentleman came to them and told them that there was neither victory nor defeat that day—as far as he could see. Both Cavaliers and Roundheads were too exhausted to carry on. Most of Rupert's Cavaliers, but not Rupert, had returned from Kineton, but they launched no second charge. An old soldier himself, a veteran of the wars in the Low Countries, he had seen the Cavalry officers ride about the field, trying to exhort their troopers to attack the Roundhead infantry. He had seen the troopers refuse. He was ashamed for them. "Too little discipline," he said once more.

It was dusk when Rupert returned with the remainder of his men. Princes Charles spied out his famous scarlet cloak from the hilltop and called to James. "Loose the dog, James! Our cousin has returned."

In spite of his gloves James's small fingers were too stiff with cold to do this. The oncoming night would be a bitter one. One of the Prince's gentlemen finally cut the dog loose with his dagger.

Boye did not wait an instant to make his farewells. Although he, too, was stiff with chill, he went down the slope at a skidding run and through the weary foot soldiers and cavalrymen as if they had not been there. He did not hear some of them cheer him as he passed. He nosed out Rupert at once, came to a stop beside him, and leaping high, barked and barked for attention. The Prince dismounted and the dog jumped, frantic with joy, upon him. If Rupert had not steadied himself against his horse, Boye would have knocked the exhausted man down. Rupert held the dog against his chest. "Happy to see me, eh? 'Tis not like Powick Bridge today, is it, lad? There we routed the Roundheads." Rupert looked over the dog's head toward the bivouac fires of the watchful enemy. "See there," he told Boye. "The enemy has not fallen back to Kineton. It seems we shall pass the night here at Edgehill like cats and mice watching one another. You shall share my cloak tonight."

Through that long cold night Boye sat with his master, sheltered by the scarlet cloak, beside a small fire. Maurice was with them; so was Will Legge. The King and young princes had sought a cold refuge in the King's coach.

The moans and piteous cries of the Roundhead and Cavalier wounded, who still lay on the battlefield between the two rows of fires, filled the horrible night, making Boye whimper and crowd closer to his master. He had not experienced such things before, but he knew that between the rows of fires there was agony and misery. He felt the urge to fill the night air, too, with his sympathetic howls.

"Poor Godforsaken devils," said Rupert gloomily. "We are having such strange weather this autumn, they will freeze to death tonight. We dare not go out and seek them for fear of the Roundheads, and the Roundheads dare not go out and take up their wounded for fear of us."

"The surgeons tell me the cold will stop the flow of blood from wounded men," Maurice hopefully told his brother.

"Much good that does a man who is freezing to death. How many have we lost?" asked Rupert.

Will Legge answered. "The King's aide told me upwards of two thousand men."

"And the Roundheads? What losses have they taken?"

"More than twice as many," replied the major.

"Ah, there's some satisfaction in that. That's fewer men we'll meet on the morrow. Then we shall beat them, eh, Boye?" said the Prince to his dog.

But there was no battle on the next day or on the next. Though Essex had four thousand fresh reinforcements come to him, the Roundhead general did not choose to fight again. He withdrew through Kineton to Warwick, opening the way to London and leaving behind to the gleeful Cava-liers seven cannon and many Roundhead flags.

Among the men who rode with the Earl of Essex on that retreat of disgrace was Trooper Elnathan Parmenter whose bitten wrist had healed well enough to permit him to wield a sword at Edgehill and to kill two of King Charles's foot soldiers. Once he had hacked his way close enough to see the King himself, but had been hurled back to his own men. Parmenter had served in the cavalry troop that had hidden itself in the hedgerows until Rupert's men had left the field. He scowled now as he rode among the others. He had seen Rupert the Robber sweep by and had cursed him, but nowhere at Edgehill had he marked out the Prince's devil of a dog. "I'll kill that white beast yet," Parmenter said aloud, making a cavalryman who rode nearby stare at him curiously.

Another Roundhead who retreated with Essex was a middle-aged captain of cavalry. His hair was worn to his shoulders, unlike that of his crop-haired companions, his nose was big, his eyes stern. The man's name was Cromwell, Oliver Cromwell. He rode mumbling to himself, too, but because he rode alone at the head of his men no one heard him. He did not speak of the witch dog. Boye did not concern him. He spoke of Rupert, and of the Roundheads. "Essex's men had no spirit! They had none at all. If we do not get men with courage, we shall be beaten again and again. Prince Rupert's men have courage, but they lack discipline. We lack spirit. I will put spirit into the men I command as well as discipline! Then, no one can stand against me!"

When one of Rupert's scouts told the Prince that Essex was abandoning Kineton, Rupert set out after the enemy with his troopers. This time because the Prince could not catch the wily Boye in time to tie him up again, the dog went too. The ice-cold wind blowing his ears back, Boye, as always avoiding flying hooves, sped through the ranks of galloping troopers. He made it to his master's side at their head, then yelped so Rupert would look down and see him.

The Prince shouted at the great dog who raced along. "You'll have to guard yourself today, my lad!"

Boye found the village of Kineton marvelously exciting. Although Essex had withdrawn most of his army, his rearguard remained. What a shouting, neighing, and barking there was when Rupert's Cavaliers thundered down on the

enemy. What a victory it was! Rupert was everywhere, bellowing orders to his men. His cavalrymen jumped over the
carts the Roundheads had hastily set up to block the way
into Kineton. With flashing swords the Cavaliers cut down
the terrified rearguard and left the enemy dead in the streets
of the village. Over all rose Rupert's voice and the deep bay
of his dog, the dog that darted among horses' legs to attack
any man who was afoot and bring him down.

" 'Tis the witch cur and the Devil Prince!" muttered
many Roundheads after they surrendered themselves rather
than stand against this fearful two.

Rupert captured the silver plates from which the Earl
of Essex dined, the earl's personal baggage, and his papers.
The plate was a great prize. It could be melted down and
sold to silversmiths to finance the Cavalier armies. The
clothing the threadbare King's troopers would wear, and the
letters and other papers would be valuable sources of military information.

With Boye at his knee, back at his camp at Edgehill,
Rupert read Essex's papers carefully. Three of the letters
brought a black scowl of anger to his face. "Have my secretary taken into custody now and brought before the King,"
he ordered his aide. Then the Prince, whose look of rage had
changed to one of sadness, took the poodle's head between
his hands. "Boye, these letters I have just read were written
by my own secretary to Lord Essex. My trusted secretary
has long sent Essex news of what I plan to do! Essex has

sent him money in exchange for information. I think the King will hang my secretary." Rupert sighed. " 'Tis a sad thing to meet with a treacherous man. You are fortunate to be a dog—and not a Prince. How few folk a Prince can trust!"

The day after this the Cavaliers broke camp at Edge-hill, and the King resumed his interrupted march on London. Rupert and Maurice went with him.

The town of Banbury surrendered to the King. Oxford, now abandoned by the Roundheads, greeted Charles again with great joy. Boye loved his entry into Oxford. He loved being with his master and hearing the pealing of Oxford's many churchbells as Rupert was acclaimed by the loyal people. Boye far preferred to walk beside Rupert's prancing horse than to ride in the King's own coach with young Charles and James. Prince James had wanted him. He had got up the courage to ask Rupert to let the dog sit beside him and stick his head out the window with James to let the people see him. The King had heard the request. He had laughingly refused to share his coach with a dog—even with such a valorous dog as the victor of Powick Bridge.

"No," the King had said. "Let the folk of Oxford see Rupert's dog entire—not only his head. Let them see all of Rupert's luck."

King Charles decided that the Cavalier army should

spend some time at Oxford and not go on to London, so
Rupert made his headquarters in Abingdon, a nearby village. He had offered to take his cavalry and ride on to London with three thousand foot soldiers and seize the strategic
places of the city. Charles's advisors opposed Rupert's bold
plan. One of the chief counselors told the King and the
others openly, "If Prince Rupert takes London, he will do
somewhat rash. He is a wild young man. I would be but
little surprised if he set the city on fire!"

The King was convinced by his overcautious advisors.
Rupert found that no amount of argument and raging at
him could change King Charles's mind. He permitted his
nephew, though, to raid for food and arms the parts of the
surrounding countryside that supported the Roundheads,
but march on London—no!

The black-browed Prince was furious. So were Maurice
and Will Legge. They always agreed with Rupert when he
beat his fists on the table in their Abingdon headquarters
and shouted, "I have the right of it! *I can take London!* I
know it! I can end this war in but one stroke!"

Boye ran about frantically during his master's outbursts,
jumping first at Rupert, then at Maurice, and finally at Will,
hoping to distract them. He knew only that he loved his
master and that his master was wretchedly unhappy.

Once Will had looked at the distraught poodle and remarked, "I do believe, Your Highness, if ye ordered it, Boye
would bite the King!"

"Sometimes I wish he would—or better yet, bite those accursed old counselors of his!" thundered the Prince. "Aye, let him bite kings—but no longer Roundheads. I must find a faithful lad to look after Boye. 'Tis not a soldier's task, so I'll not ask a trooper or my aide!"

Will told the Prince gravely, "Do that, or the dog will surely come to grief. At Powick Bridge he might have been shot. At Kineton he was in much danger—and only by a miracle not harmed."

After his outburst against the King, Rupert did not mention a serving boy again. Occupied with their own problems, Will and Maurice did not think to remind him. But one winter's night, chilled, exhausted, and footsore, a lad came to the Prince's headquarters. His cloak was stained and torn, his face white, and his large eyes staring. It was Hugh Joliffe, who had at last been sent home to England by the English ambassador at Vienna. The boy had finally been able to convince the man that he had promise of employment with Prince Rupert. The ambassador had not been sorry to give Hugh money out of his own pocket and let him go. The page, since his return from Linz, had been a boasting, disturbing influence in his household.

Sometimes begging, sometimes paying his way Hugh had crossed France by farm cart, coach, and on foot. He had concealed himself on a ship that sailed from Calais to England and had not been discovered until they docked in Dover. There he had been beaten by the angry ship captain,

but all the same set ashore in England. From Dover Hugh
had made his way to London, seeking Rupert. Unchallenged
by the Roundheads in London because of his youth, the boy
had learned that Rupert was at Oxford, some fifty miles
away. Hugh had walked from London to the King's headquarters, and there had been told to seek the Prince at
Abingdon.

Will Legge, who did not know him, refused to admit
him to the Prince. "A beggar lad," he told Maurice, who had
come up to him while he questioned Hugh. "I find it passing
strange that a beggar lad would come to *us* when we live off
what the countryside offers us and have little to spare!"

"Perhaps he's a Roundhead spy?" suggested the Prince's
brother. "The Roundheads would employ a little lad!"

"Perhaps he's even an assassin?" commented Legge
with his ringing laugh.

"What is your name, boy?" Maurice asked. "Why do
you seek Prince Rupert?"

Hugh removed his hat, bowed unsteadily, and said,
"Hugh Joliffe. I once. . . ."

"Joliffe?" Maurice's look was one of astonishment. His
mouth had fallen open. "I know that name, Joliffe. Are you
the serving lad who was with my brother at Linz?"

"I served Prince Rupert there," replied the boy. He
managed to smile. "Then you are Prince Maurice, my master's brother? Folk in London spoke of you."

Maurice took the boy by the arm and started toward

the stairs to go above to the inn rooms where Rupert lodged, but at the bottom of the steps Hugh fainted from fatigue and hunger. Maurice caught him before he fell, lifted him, and carried him to his brother's door. He kicked it open and strode in, the unconscious page in his arms.

Rupert had been standing over the table carefully scrutinizing maps. Alarmed by the sudden interruption, the Prince reached for a primed pistol near him, but seeing Maurice, at once put it down. Boye, asleep by Rupert's chair, woke up, and got to his feet.

"Maurice, when will you ever rap before you enter? Someday I may shoot you!" exclaimed Rupert. Then he saw the boy in his brother's arms. "What in the name of the devil do you have there?" Before Maurice could reply, Prince Rupert crossed his chamber to see Maurice's burden more closely. One glance was enough for him to recognize his page. "My God, Maurice, it is the little serving lad from Vienna! He looks like death itself. How did he come here from Austria? What ails him?"

Maurice answered, "He is ill. What am I to do with him?"

"Put him on my bed, then go ask Will Legge to find a physician."

While Boye came over to see, Maurice put Hugh Joliffe on his master's bed, then hurried out.

Rupert bent over the unconscious boy, taking Hugh's cold hands in his.

The dog pressed close to Rupert until Hugh's scent came to his nose. Boye stood, sniffing it. A memory came back to him—an evil memory. He had known this scent before. It was hateful. As Rupert spoke to the page, the poodle's growl of suspicion arose, a deep rumbling one from his chest, but his master's hand pushed Boye off roughly when the dog would have leaped up onto the bed too.

"Do not grumble, Boye! 'Tis little Joliffe," the Prince ordered in the angry tone the dog disliked. " 'Tis Hugh! He's come back to me when I thought he could not."

Chapter VII

Spies

THE OLD PHYSICIAN from Abingdon took Hugh's pulse, peered at his tongue, and lifted his eyelids. Then he declared, "He is exhausted, Your Highness. I shall take him into my house if you choose." The physician gave Rupert a sourish glance, for his brother's farm had been raided by Rupert's men. "I do not imagine that you would be able to tend to him. You seem to have much to occupy your time."

"No," replied the Prince. "I do not see how I can easily tend to the lad to whom I owe so much." He looked tenderly at the page. "I will pay you well, never fear, for the care you give him. When he is well, he shall serve me again. Am I to visit him?"

The physician shook his head. "No, Your Highness." He

hesitated for a moment, looking at Boye who stood behind Rupert, his lips lifted in a soundless snarl because of Hugh's unwelcome presence. Then the man asked, "May I speak openly to you?"

"Aye, you may."

"I am not by sympathy a Cavalier, Your Highness—nor is my wife. We could scarce entertain you with a good con-science."

Rupert smiled slightly. "Aye, what would the neighbors think?" Then he nodded his assent. "I shall not come then. But tell the lad he shall serve me soon."

The physician went toward the door. "Have someone fetch the lad down for me, well wrapped against the night air. My coach is below."

"I'll bring him to you myself." Taking a coverlet from his bed, the Prince wrapped Hugh Joliffe in it and left the room. He closed the door behind him on Boye's suspicious nose so the dog could not follow him.

Deeply offended, not only by his master's behavior but by this scent he detested, Boye yelped and flung his weight against the heavy door. The fifth time he rammed it he burst it open and ran out onto the stairway. There, as he bounded down, he met Rupert coming up. The Prince smacked him playfully on the rump.

Rupert was in high spirits. "Boye, 'tis plain to see you have no memory anymore of Linz Castle! 'Twas more than a year ago we left Austria. Now Hugh's come to me again.

Before long I believe that you'll love him as much as ever you did!"

The page remained at the physician's for some weeks, and in that time Boye and Rupert kept themselves occupied while they waited for the King to make up his mind to march on London. Rupert fought a skirmish at Aylesbury, but this time he left Boye behind, locked, wretched, inside the inn chamber.

Some days later, to the dog's joy, the restless Prince decided to go out again spying, a thing he delighted in. After the battle of Edgehill Lord Essex had retreated to the town of Warwick with the main body of his army. Rupert decided he would visit Warwick some forty miles to the north. "Boye comes!" he told the dog.

Rupert donned a plain snuff-colored cloth coat borrowed from Will Legge and the usual black steeple hat worn by villagers, then told Maurice and Will to disguise Boye.

"How shall we do *that?*" asked Will.

"With ashes. Rub gray ashes into his coat well. A gray dog he'll be this day!"

The two princes and Legge rubbed the white poodle from head to tail with ashes from the hearthfire. At Rupert's command Boye stayed, though the powdery stuff made him sneeze again and again. Finally he was as Rupert had said, a gray dog.

The Prince mounted the sorry old nag Maurice had found for him and with Boye walking at its side left Abingdon for the north. Not a soul, not even passing troopers of his own command, recognized him, for he kept his head down as a humble countryman would before such dashing Cavaliers. They went, unchallenged, through the countryside.

Some eight miles out of Warwick, it began to rain. "We'll seek shelter, my lad," the shivering Prince told Boye. "It would not do for you to lose your fine gray coat before we brave my Lord of Essex's camp."

Rupert and Boye went into a conveniently found alehouse and sat before the hearth drying themselves. Only one other traveler was in the common room, a seller of nets to put about cabbages to bring them to market. Rupert opened a conversation with him. "What would yer business be?"

"To sell my nets in Warwick. But my horse, curse her, took lame," the stranger replied glumly.

"Let me sell them for you! I go to Warwick myself."

"How do I know ye will not steal my cabbage nets?" The stranger eyed Rupert suspiciously.

"I will pay ye for them now. Then they'll be mine. Tell me their worth."

"Nine shillings," replied the other traveler.

"Agreed," Rupert told him, and counted out nine shillings from his old purse. "When the rain stops I'll take my-

self to Warwick with my nets. In the meantime, friend, let
me buy ye a second tankard of ale."

An hour later the rain ceased so the Prince and Boye
went on their way again over the puddle-filled road.

Warwick was a small place, swarming with Roundhead
soldiers, none of whom took any note of the cabbage-net
seller who rode slowly about with the large gray dog at his
nag's heels. The Roundheads did not plant cabbages. They
had no interest in the shabbily dressed dark young man who
carefully examined all of the entryways into Warwick while
he hawked and sold his farm wares. Some few folk took
second glances at Boye. One or two remarked on his unusual breed and his great size and idly wondered where the
countryman had come by such an animal, but no one recognized him as the terrible witch dog.

The only man who might have marked him out through
his coat of ashes was absent from Essex's camp that day.
Elnathan Parmenter had prevailed upon the captain of his
troop to permit him to go out spying, himself. Parmenter's
wife had lived in Abingdon before coming to Surrey, where
she had met and married him. He had several times visited
the town with her and knew the countryside around it.
When he had learned that Rupert the Robber was there, he
resolved to go to Abingdon. He put aside his somber clothing for a worn green-gray velvet coat and a captured Cavalier hat. He did not fear being recognized in his wife's birth-
place, for it was some years since he had been there.

In Abingdon he counted the numbers and the strength of Rupert's forces, then set himself down in a tavern to overhear whatever he could. Two Cavaliers came in and sat very near him. Over cups of wine they spoke freely—but not of military matters.

"Have ye heard how the serving lad fares? The lad who came so far to serve the Prince?" the one with red moustaches asked the other.

"Aye, they say he mends readily enough at the house of Physician Cotterell, who is a good leech—though a Round-head. Soon the boy will join Rupert. The clack is that he will tend to Rupert's luck," came from the second Cavalier, a man in a scarlet coat.

"To look after the dog, eh? Would that I had a lad to look after my mount!" the first man remarked. Then he began to speak of how often his horse ailed and how little the local farriers had helped him.

Elnathan had harkened carefully to their words about the page and particularly carefully to their comments about Boye. Physician Cotterell had once treated his wife and wife's family. Parmenter already knew that Cotterell was of his Roundhead sympathies. He had not needed the words of the Cavaliers to learn that. Leaving a farthing behind for his beer, he got up and left the tavern. Why not pay a call on the good physician? he asked himself. Why not learn what military information he could from the man? He need not tell Cotterell that he was a trooper in Lord Essex's army. The old physician would not guess it.

Cotterell, however, was not at home. But Goodwife Cotterell remembered Elnathan Parmenter, who told her he came from London to buy salt beef in the Abingdon market. She sniffed at his strange clothing and was not about to let him inside until he told her that he had been informed in London that if he garbed himself as a Cavalier he would not be molested in Rupert the Robber's camp. Once inside, she served him cheese, bread, and October ale. Within a few minutes it was clear to Parmenter that the physician's old wife took no notice of military matters. She preferred to gossip of people, so he asked of her husband and her grown children. Then they spoke of the disgusting behavior of the Cavaliers and the chill unseasonable weather.

"Aye, Master Parmenter," she replied when he brought the talk around to the page at last. "He is a likely lad, thir' teen years of age." She leaned forward to speak more softly. "Far too fine he is to serve Rupert the Devil! Hugh has the face of an angel and the manners to match!"

"He is to tend to the Prince's cur, I'm told, goodwife."

The woman sighed. The sound was of relief. "That is good news to me. If he busies himself with the beast, he may not so often be near the Prince."

"Mistress Cotterell, the dog is ever with Rupert," Parmenter told her gravely. "Must the lad go to Prince Rupert, do you think? He is no slave, bound to that Devil's evil service."

"My husband has also bethought himself of that. He has spoken to the lad, but to no avail. He is strong willed."

"What does the child say then?"

"That he came from Austria for one cause alone—to seek out Prince Rupert and to serve him as he had served him when he was a prisoner. Would that Devil were still a prisoner!"

"Aye, Goodwife." Parmenter took a sip of ale and asked, "I am curious about the lad. Do you think I would be permitted to see him? Is he well enough?"

"He lies still abed, sir, but my husband permits me to speak with him. I think the lad is lonely. It will do him no harm to speak with someone else. My husband would not care overmuch if you visited the page, I think. Come with me, Master Parmenter."

She got up from her table and led the way up the stairs to a door, pushing it open to let Parmenter enter before her. Hugh Joliffe lay in bed, propped up with pillows, a small book in his hand.

Goodwife Cotterell said cheerily, "I have fetched someone to see you, Hugh. This is Master Parmenter. He wishes to speak with you. I shall leave you here, master. I must see to my maids who churn today." The woman smiled and went out then.

Parmenter, with Hugh's unblinking eyes upon him, pulled a chair up to the bed and sat down, smiling.

"You come from the Prince?" were Hugh's first words.

"No, my lad. I am friend to the Cotterells. I came here to visit them today and was told of you."

The boy was clearly disappointed. "Rupert has *not* come to me," he said angrily.

"The Prince is a busy man," Parmenter told him in his soft manner. "Too, Physician Cotterell favors the cause of the Parliament. Cavaliers are not welcome in this house."

"Oh." Hugh was more easy now that he had heard this. He put his book down onto the coverlet, and Parmenter picked it up. It was from Cotterell's library, a book of sermons much favored by him.

Parmenter detested the name the enemy gave to the army of Parliament, but now he used it. "These are Roundhead sermons, my lad. Are you of that persuasion?"

Hugh didn't look at his questioner. He gazed out the window at the gray November sky. "I have lived in Vienna for as long as I can remember. I know little of England. Roundheads or Cavaliers?" He shrugged. "What are they? I do not truly know."

"Yet you choose to serve Prince Rupert? Why, if you are not a Cavalier, would you do that?"

Hugh Joliffe laughed, but there was no music in it. "Because I once served him in Austria. He is my master. Because he is a Prince!"

Parmenter's question was sly. "It pleases you to serve a Prince?"

"Aye, what page would not choose a Prince over a merchant or any other man?" Hugh turned his head and looked coldly and significantly at Parmenter.

"No servant lad that I have ever known," the Round-head agreed, then added, "but, 'twill not be the Prince you serve."

"What?" Hugh sat up in the bed. Some color rose into his face, a flush of anger, Parmenter noted.

"I have heard the tavern talk. You will care for Rupert's dog."

Hugh fell back onto his pillows while Parmenter care-fully watched his telltale face. The boy was scowling, his brows drawn tight together as he clenched his fists, but he said no word.

"You do not fancy the Prince's dog, Hugh?" asked the man.

"No," Hugh burst out. "Boye! 'Tis *always* Boye. I came here to England to serve the Prince—not his Austrian cur, that dog who bit me!"

Parmenter thought with satisfaction—the page also hates the white dog. He said, "I am told that Prince Rupert and the King soon will march on London."

Though Parmenter had hoped Hugh might add some re-mark to his comment, the boy seemed little interested. "Will they?"

"That is what folk say. If you tend to Rupert's dog, you will journey to London with the Cavaliers, I suspect. When my business is done here, I will return to London. Perhaps I will see you again there when the Cavaliers take the city as I know they will."

"Aye." Hugh replied without enthusiasm. He looked

out the window again and did not turn his head as his visitor got up, went out, and closed the door softly behind him.

Parmenter stopped at the head of the stairway. He was nodding as he quietly said to himself, "Yes, I shall see that lad again, the page who tends to Rupert's demon of a cur."

That evening two horsemen passed each other during a snowstorm.

Rupert, his poodle by his side, contentedly rode south to Abingdon with intelligence of the roads into and out of Warwick.

Parmenter jogged along north to Warwick, his head filled with thoughts of Hugh Joliffe and the dog they both hated, wondering how best to turn this knowledge to his advantage. And at last a plan came to him. He gnawed his lower lip thinking of it. It would require the aid and agreement of his troop captain, but Parmenter did not think this would be difficult to secure.

Because of the falling snow the two men saw one another only as shadows, somewhat darker than the sky. The Roundhead did not mark out the dog at all. Boye's coat of ashes was gone by now, blown away by the brisk wind and washed away by a chill downpour just outside Warwick.

The poodle was his white self again and against the white road nearly invisible.

* * *

Hugh was brought back to his master by Physician Cotterell three days before King Charles finally made up his
mind to leave Oxford with his army for London.

How Boye disliked the return of the page! He
crouched, wary, beside the Prince's bed, guarding it, as
Rupert and Maurice greeted the boy. The poodle knew better than to snarl while his master was present, but not for a
moment did he take his eyes from the page he hated.

Hugh bowed, smiling, before Rupert. "I have come
back to you as I promised, Your Highness."

"And I am heartily glad to see you," Rupert told him.
"You have come afar by yourself. Tell me of Vienna and the
ambassador."

"They are unchanged. Things Austrian do not change,
master." Hugh glanced meaningfully at Boye. "Am I to tend
the *pudelhund* again?"

"You are. Boye is your chief care from this moment.
Watch him well," Rupert told the page with a laugh.

Hugh replied quietly, "Aye, master, he shall be well
watched."

"You are to share my lodgings at night for a time,"
announced Maurice.

A quick shadow of fury crossed Hugh's face, then he
asked, "Why is that, Your Highness? At Linz Castle I had a
bed in my master's chamber."

"Tell him, Rupert," prompted a laughing Maurice.
"Tell him. I refuse to do this."

Rupert seemed almost embarrassed, then shook his

head and said, " 'Tis Boye, Joliffe. The dog is jealous of all newcomers. I heard his grumble when you were first brought here. It will take time for Boye to accept you again. Dogs do not remember as well as do loyal lads."

Hugh glanced once more at Boye.

The dog, hearing his master speak his name, had got to his feet, hoping Rupert would say "Come Boye." When the Prince did not, the poodle sat down and began to scratch an annoying flea, but still he watched the page.

"Take heart, Joliffe," Maurice remarked. "The news is that we march on London within a few days. You will not long suffer my snoring. You will travel to London with the Cavaliers. There will be a place for you in the baggage carts among the extra equipment and the provender."

"What provender?" demanded Rupert almost gaily. "We live off the countryside. Tell me, lad," he said to Hugh, "have you ever entered a Roundhead hen house in the dark of the moon and taken a plump hen?"

Hugh either did not see the joke or did not choose to see it. "For you, master," he replied, as gravely as if he had been asked to perform some weighty task, "I would do any-thing!"

"Then, know this, lad. You must keep Boye from going into battle! It is a great concern for me."

"Someday he would surely be killed," Maurice said.

"Aye," Hugh agreed. "Someday he well could be!"

And once more Hugh Joliffe looked Boye's way.

* * *

In drizzly late-autumn weather the King broke up his Oxford camp and slowly moved his army eastwards, Rupert and his Cavaliers riding ahead of Charles's soldiers, scouting.

During the days Boye was happy, because then he trotted beside his master's horse, but at night on the march he was miserable. At that time Rupert was always occupied, conferring with the King. Maurice and Will Legge went with him, but the whimpering poodle was now left behind with Hugh. The dog slept, tied, in the baggage cart on a mattress near Hugh or behind locked doors in some chamber. Joliffe this time fed Boye because the page feared inquisitive eyes now that he was among English folk to whom the dog was important, but night after night he sat staring at the poodle, wondering how best to rid himself of him.

The page had heard much talk since he joined Rupert of the Roundhead opinion that Boye was a witch dog. Now he asked himself how he could turn this to his advantage? He did not once think of Elnathan Parmenter, the merchant, who had said he returned to London, and who had promised he would see him again.

Parmenter thought, however, of Hugh. The Earl of Essex had taken his army on into London. Parmenter had gone there riding with his troop. When they arrived he sought an interview with his captain, Josiah Addison, and told Addison of Rupert's page.

"And what of that lad?" Addison had asked. He was a busy, quick-tempered man with reddish hair, a high voice, and a small mouth. "What is a servant lad to us? Will he wield a sword for Rupert?"

"No, 'tis not that I came here to speak of. 'Tis of the witch dog of the Prince's."

"Aye, ye told me the lad's to tend to the cur."

"Captain, you know what our men say of this beast Rupert fetched out of Germany with him—that he's fed on human flesh, children's flesh, and that he can become invisible when he chooses."

Addison growled, "Foolishness! Superstition! I believe not a word of it—nor should you, Parmenter."

"Parliament's soldiers do, though, sir. What if they were to learn the truth—that the witch dog is but a common animal? Would they then fear Prince Rupert so much? They call him Devil now and his dog a demon and his familiar. What if they learn that the white beast is as plain a cur as any cur in England and that Rupert is but a man like any other man? He fights skirmish after skirmish and not a hair of his head is harmed. They say this is because of his 'luck'! They would fight better if they knew this to be untrue."

Josiah Addison looked at the chart spread out before him. "Aye, there is sense in what you say. Something worth the pondering here. What do ye plot?" The captain knew the man before him well.

"The page hates the dog! He would sell him to us. This

I believe. I ask to be given this task when the King approaches London. I told the serving lad I'd see him when he comes with his master here. He did not believe me but will remember me, I know."

The Roundhead captain nodded. "As you wish."

He picked up his quill and dipped it into the ink. "I give you the letter you require now. Ride west and meet the Cavaliers who approach London. I leave all to you, trooper, but bring me the witch dog. Bring him alive."

"Alive?" Parmenter was surprised at this.

"What is a dead dog to me, trooper? Only a few superstitious fools would view a dead animal. A live one could be seen for many days—if he were caged. Every man in our armies could view him. Now," Addison stood up, "I have done all for you that I shall do. Until you accomplish your task, you are alone. I have but one more soldier's labor for you. Tell this Captain Cromwell, who waits outside my chamber, to enter."

Dismissed, Parmenter left. He greeted Captain Oliver Cromwell and told him to go in, then hurried on downstairs. Too elated to take much note of the other man, the trooper did not see how Cromwell looked after him, frowning his distaste at Parmenter's dirty clothing and his slack unsoldierly manner.

Boye found the approach to London a dismal one. He never spent one night in the same place. The Prince and his troopers rode from fine Roundhead house to fine house, smashing furniture and windows, carrying off the feather-beds and books. Rupert did not try over hard to restrain them—though he did not permit them to abuse children or women. The Prince knew this looting was the way of soldiers. It was a thing he had often seen when he fought in Europe.

Rupert went to meet the King on Hounslow Heath some miles from London. Boye accompanied him and saw his master actually tear his hair in exasperation and shout at the King. Maurice and two others held the dog, so he would not attack the King's old advisors when Rupert shook his fist at them.

Boye was present, too, when the King gave his permission for Rupert's cavalry to push on again—to Brentford. Boye did not go, however. He stayed behind with the main part of the Cavalier army, sitting sorrowfully beneath the baggage wagon.

The battle of Brentford was no glorious Powick Bridge. The day was so foggy beside the River Thames that Boye could have seen nothing but the legs of the horses about him. He would have found it an odd combat. The town was barricaded against the Cavaliers, and Roundhead guns thundered their welcome to Rupert's men. The Prince's mounted troopers could not go forward, so Rupert commanded foot soldiers to take the town. "For God and King,"

they shouted, as they shoved the Roundheads back so cavalry could leap the barricades and rout them. Three regiments of Roundhead foot soldiers retreated east toward
London.

During a lull in the battle Maurice rode to his brother,
calling out, "The Roundheads flee into the Thames!"

Rupert's laugh rang clear. "I would that Boye were
here. He could retrieve the vermin for me. We have had a
good day's hunting. Brentford is ours!"

"Shall we meet the enemy again tomorrow, Rupert?"

"I pray that we shall at the very gates of London. Now
let us secure the town we've taken. I've sent my aide to take
the news to our uncle."

While the Prince's aide galloped to the King, Hugh
Joliffe, waiting with Boye, received an unexpected visitor.
Parmenter the Roundhead, dressed much as before, appeared out of the fog. He knew the Cavalier watchword. A
man loyal to the King had been captured early that day
while he scouted ahead of the army. This spy had told Captain Addison what the watchword was, and Addison had at
once sent a message to Parmenter. The Roundhead trooper
used it fearlessly, was admitted to the King's camp and di-
rected to Rupert's carts where he found the Prince's serving
lad.

Hugh came down out of the cart at the man's call. "Yes,
I recall you, Master Parmenter," he told the Roundhead spy,
who looked only once at Hugh and kept his gaze on the dog
below the cart.

A nervous Parmenter came directly to the point. Many Cavaliers were moving about in the mist, some of them perilously close to him. "Ye hate the dog, do you not, the dog which bit ye?"

"Aye."

"What if I told ye he had bitten me, too? Look at my wrist." The man showed it to the page.

Hugh examined the still-red toothmarks and nodded. "It does not surprise me."

"What if I took the cur off your hands?" Parmenter asked. "What would ye say to that?"

"Good riddance, 'tis what I would say. What would you do with him?" Hugh's face had grown animated now. "Will you kill him? Will you take him far away from here and kill him, so the Prince will never know?" Hugh looked about him, too, at the nearby Cavaliers, then got down on his hands and knees to peer under the cart where the mournful dog lay, waiting for his master to return.

Boye growled at him and the page got up to face Parmenter. "I'll deliver him to you, Master Parmenter, at dawn. There is an inn not far from here, the Crown and Shield. My master will sleep heavily tonight, but I will not sleep. The fog will last through the night, I think." Hugh paused, then went on, "I know where the sentries are. I can slip by them with the dog. If you give me your promise to kill him, I'll come to you."

"I'll give ye thirty shillings for the savage beast," offered the trooper.

Hugh shook his head. "No, I'll not sell this dog. I'll *give* him to you." Hugh smiled. "You do be a Roundhead, I think?"

Taken aback by the baldness of the question, Parmenter hesitated, fearful, but Hugh spoke before he did. " 'Tis of no matter to me, Master Parmenter. It pleases me that you are. Now I *know* you will kill this dog. Do not fail me at the Crown and Shield."

"I shall not," promised Parmenter, who then turned and left.

Chapter **VIII**

London Town

THE NEWS the Prince's aide brought from Brentford to the King's camp on Hounslow Heath was very welcome.

Boye heard the drum of hooves, saw the rider come out of the heavy mists, and heard his shout. The dog got up at once and stood waiting. Was it Rupert? He heard the glad cries of the Cavaliers and saw Hugh fling himself out of the cart to run to the rider.

"The Prince is not harmed?" demanded the page, clinging to the excited aide's stirrup.

"Nay, lad, not even scratched. He has taken Brentford!"

"Does he come here now?" Hugh's question was an eager one.

The aide shook his head. "No, he lies tonight at Brentford."

"Does he fight tomorrow?"

"Rupert thinks he will. The Roundheads that the Prince drove from their barricades have regrouped at Turn-ham Green to face us. Reinforcements come from London to join them."

The page had heard enough. Rupert would *not* be back that night. The way was clear to dispose of the dog. Hugh went back and peered under the cart to make sure Boye was still tied to the heavy wheel. He laughed, but fell silent when the dog's hackles rose and his growl began.

Hugh did not sleep that night. He found it easy to stay awake because of the cold. When the fog about the heath changed from black to dawn's whitish-gray, he got down from the cart and untied the poodle. Boye was eager to run from him but too stiff with the damp cold to pull hard enough to break away from the determined page. Delib-erately Hugh choked him with the collar, cutting off his breath so he could not bark.

The two set out across the heath in an eastward direc-tion through the mists. Once through a gap in them Hugh saw a sentry. He was afraid and threw himself down onto the wet grass as the sentry paced by. Then lad and white dog slipped past.

A half hour after they had passed the sentry unseen, the page and the nearly throttled animal arrived at the door of the Crown and Shield, an old half-timbered, thatch-roofed country inn, a goodly distance north of the main road to London. Standing before its door, Hugh called out softly, "Master Parmenter!"

The Roundhead trooper had waited at the inn through out the night, sitting on by its warm hearth when the inn keeper had gone up to bed. Now at the boy's cry, he came out at once, shutting the door silently behind him so he would not be seen with the Prince's servant.

Parmenter looked at Boye in a satisfied manner. How easily he had procured his wish, and it had cost him not a farthing. Captain Addison would be pleased with him. He would favor him above the other men of his command now. The Roundhead moved toward Boye.

The dog sprang back, snarling and snapping. Boye had his scent now. He did not remember the trooper or what had happened at Powick Bridge, but he disliked this man.

"Hold the beast!" commanded Parmenter, who took a pistol from the large deep pocket of his coat.

"I cannot," Hugh gasped out, as he was pulled down by Boye's sudden lunge forward at the Roundhead. The leather rope was suddenly drawn through the page's grabbing hands as the poodle sprang at Parmenter. "Shoot him!" cried the boy.

Parmenter had no such intention. As the white dog hurtled past him, he swerved to one side and brought down his pistol on top of the dog's head. Boye fell limp to the ground, breaking through the thin film of ice covering a large puddle before the inn door.

"He's dead! *You've killed him!*" Hugh exclaimed, his face aglow with joy.

Parmenter put his finger to his lips. "Keep your voice down. The innkeeper must not hear us. He is a Cavalier, I think!" The trooper squatted to feel Boye's chest. "His heart beats. See how his sides heave. The dog is but stunned."

"But you'll kill him still?"

"Aye, ye have my promise on that, but 'twill not be done here. I cannot risk a pistol being heard. I have a hay cart behind the inn, hired last night from a farmer." Par-menter grinned. "The dog will be bound and placed in that —under the hay I'll take to London to feed Essex's horses. There I'll shoot this demon dog. Now be off with ye, lad. Ye must not be found missing."

Hugh looked hard and long at Boye, who lay senseless, the puddle's brown water staining his white coat. Then the page glanced once at Parmenter, gave the Roundhead a twisted smile, and darted away.

Parmenter watched him until he was gone, lost in the white mists. He put his pistol away, took out a knife from his cuff, and cut the leash from the dog's collar. It was long enough, he had decided, long enough to bind the witch dog's great legs tight together.

Rupert did not come back to Hounslow Heath that day. When he did somewhat later he was a grim man. The Roundheads had, indeed, taken up a position at Turnham

Green. Their forces there had greatly outnumbered the King's. When the mists evaporated on that Sunday, the thirteenth of November, the Cavaliers had gaped in amazement to see the hordes of soldiers who had poured out of London to save the city.

Rupert charged fiercely but fruitlessly. Then, for a day the two armies stood at a standstill, gazing at one another. King Charles at last decided it would be folly to attack so many with so few. During the night he withdrew his army again to the heath.

Lord Essex's soldiers pursued the Cavaliers as they retreated. In spite of Rupert's desperate defense of Brentford the next day, he was driven out by the Roundheads and he, too, fell back on Hounslow Heath. The young Prince was not accustomed to defeat. He was in a black mood when he rode into his uncle's camp with Maurice and Will Legge.

All three sat dejectedly in their saddles. Only Maurice was able to manage a smile when Hugh came running through the rain to his master.

"Your Highness! Your Highness!" he cried out. "The dog has run away from me!"

Rupert's face grew even blacker. He reached down and roughly dragged Hugh up onto his horse before him. "How the devil did it happen?" he demanded.

"Master, the poodle gnawed through his tether and in the night ran away." Hugh was genuinely frightened of the Prince in this temper and burst into tears.

"Have you sought him through the camp?" asked Will Legge.

"Aye, I have," choked out the page, telling the truth. He had felt this action would be wise of him, for it would cover his treachery. "No man's seen him. He's disappeared."

"He ran away to find you no doubt, Rupert," suggested Maurice. "When he doesn't find you, he'll come back."

"Boye will come back," added Legge, trying to comfort the Prince. " 'Tis not the lad's fault. He must sleep some-time."

Rupert set the page onto the ground, then looked up into the sky, his head thrown back, the icy rain running in streaks down his hardened face. "This is a foul day," he said as calmly as if he were admiring a fine one. "I've lost Brent-ford and I've lost my 'luck,' it seems." With these words he turned his horse and rode slowly toward the center of the camp where the King made his headquarters.

Gravely Will looked after Rupert. "He's lost more than his 'luck,' I think. He's lost something he loved. I do not think your brother is a man who gives his heart easily. Boye had long been with him. If he does not return, no other dog can take his place."

Maurice nodded. "It seems a folly to talk of an animal when a town's been lost to the enemy, and many brave men have died, but somehow I do not find it so. I pray Boye will come back. Rupert has need of him."

It was Will's turn to nod. Then the two officers, the

white plumes in their hats sodden with rain, also moved away to cross the heath, following Rupert.

Neither of them saw Hugh Joliffe smile as he went jauntily back through the downpour to the shelter of the baggage cart and the comfort of his coverlets.

Boye did not come back. The Prince offered a fine reward and ordered all Cavalier scouting parties to keep a sharp eye for him, but no man saw him. When King Charles decided some days later that he would now seek winter quarters for his army, the Prince reluctantly abandoned the search and glumly rode away again to Abingdon. He spoke little on the march to either his brother or to Will, and they did not mention the missing poodle to him.

Hugh also kept silent. He stayed out of Rupert's way as much as possible while the Cavalier army was encamped on Hounslow Heath, afraid he might be out of his master's favor. Perhaps the Prince would blame him because the poodle had got loose? Hugh sat in the cart for hours, a damp coverlet about his shoulders, chewing on his nails, wondering what Rupert was thinking.

His thoughts were at last set at rest when they reached Abingdon. There the Prince spoke after supper to his page. "You are all that remains to me, Joliffe, of my years in Austria. Now that Boye has run away and you have nothing to tend but myself, do you wish to leave me?"

"No, master! I came to England to serve *you!*" Boldly

Hugh spoke the words he had rehearsed on the westward march from Hounslow Heath, hoping Rupert would say this to him. "I did not come to England to serve your *pudelhund,* but because you required it of me, I did it willingly."

"And you did it well."

Hugh smiled. "I am pleased, Your Highness, that you are not angry with me because the *pudelhund* ran away."

"No, Hugh," said the Prince. He sounded weary as he stared down at his boots. " 'Twas not your fault. Boye was always fractious when I rode out and he was left behind." Rupert lifted his head and looked into the page's pretty face. "So you will serve *me,* eh!"

"For as long as you'll have me, Your Highness."

"I'll have you then," Rupert told him, clapping him on the shoulder, "until you're grown tall enough to be a trooper. Will you still serve me in my cavalry?"

"Aye, master, I will—though I die for it. I grow tall now, taller than most boys here in Abingdon who are my age."

"So you do, so you do," said the Prince almost in a whisper. His eyes were no longer on the lad but on the hearthfire flames.

Boye came into London by the north road, bound and lying almost suffocated under the hay, over which was a heavy weatherproof cloth. He heard Parmenter's cursing and the screeching of cart wheels on cobbled streets. The dog felt the jolting of the cart as it came to a sharp halt before the troop headquarters, a Cavalier's fine house that had been confiscated. When the Roundhead leaped down, Boye heard the rushing sound of boots as he ran to tell Captain Addison of his great success.

The poodle tried to bark but under the hay and the cloth, the sound was too muffled to be heard. He lay, helpless, in pain from the blow of the pistol. He could move his legs back and forth together as if he were running, but he could not stand. Boye could do nothing but gasp for air and listen. He soon heard Parmenter's and Addison's excited voices beside the cart.

A few moments later the weatherproof cloth was removed. Neither Roundhead cared whether or not the hay would be ruined in the fine rain. It had served its purpose. Rupert the Devil's dog was far more important to them than fodder for cavalry horses. Both men clambered up into the cart, and Parmenter began to claw away the hay to expose the prize.

The trooper pulled away the last of the hay, then stood gloating over his prisoner. Boye saw the men the instant they saw him and tried once more to struggle to his feet, but without success.

Addison laughed. "Before God, it *is* Rupert's dog! I remember him well from that day at Powick Bridge." The captain took command at once. "Parmenter, send for troopers to carry him belowstairs. He's to be locked in the cellar

and a guard to be stationed before the door. Then hie yourself to our troop blacksmith."

Parmenter nodded and grinned. They had discussed
this before. "To construct a cage, captain?"

"The very thing!" Josiah Addison told him.

The cellar of Addison's headquarters was cold, black,
wet, and evil smelling. Addison's men, unwilling to touch
Boye, were not gentle with him. Four troopers held him
down while the captain sliced the thongs about his feet.
Addison cut him. When Boye yelped in pain, the man
kicked him, cursed him, and called him "filthy cur." Finally
he fastened the dog, who had been so cramped by his captivity that he could scarcely move, to a post with an iron
chain.

"Now," Boye heard the captain tell his troopers, "you
see that this is but a dog. You have laid hands on him, the
dog you call a witch dog, and you are still alive, are you
not? Look well at the cur. All of Essex's army will soon view
him—in a cage. He is but a beast. You have been told he can
become invisible at will. Did he just now? He has no magic
powers—none at all—no more than his master, Prince
Rupert. Someday, ere long, we may see that Devil himself in
a cage."

After the first hours Boye did not howl, though he
spent three long days in the cellar.

He was not alone. Rats infested the house. They added to his misery as they ran across his body when he tried to sleep on the chill, wet floor. He could not see them to catch them in his jaws, and they came, squeaking, to torment him constantly and to eat the food the Roundheads tossed him.

At first when the cellar door was opened for a chunk of meat to be thrown through it, Boye had rushed his enemies —as far as the length of his chain would permit. After he had hurt his throat twice, he gave this up and remained sitting, blinking at the brightness of their candle lights while he snarled his defiance.

At the beginning of his confinement the meat they gave him was half-rotted and his water taken from the filthy trough in the center of the street. Captain Addison, however, soon put a stop to that when he smelled the meat a trooper brought past him one day on his way to the cellar. "The dog is to be kept alive, you dolts! Give him clean water from the conduit and good meat—but not too much of either. We want the cur hale but not too strong. Whatever— he must not die."

"Aye," agreed Parmenter, who stood beside the captain as his undisputed favorite now, "the dog must not die—not yet."

On the fourth day the good-sized cage was at last ready. The troop blacksmith had it fetched on a cart to Addison's headquarters. The captain and Parmenter hurried down to the square before the London house to examine it.

Parmenter tried to move its bars apart; then Addison attempted it also.

"Ye'll find it a goodly piece of work," the smith told them proudly. "It would hold fast the devil himself!"

"So it shall," Addison remarked. Then he turned to the troopers who guarded the house. "Bring forth the dog!"

They hastened to obey his command. When they had gone inside to the cellar, the captain reached into his pocket and took out a large padlock. He handed it to the black-smith, saying to him and to Parmenter, "I shall have the only key to this. Unless I unlock the cage, no other man shall. And I do not have it in mind to do this. The beast is vicious."

"When the dog has served his purpose, what will ye do with him?" asked the curious blacksmith.

"Kill him," said Parmenter.

"Aye," the captain agreed. "What use then would we have for him?"

Boye heard the men coming for him. He backed as far as he could into a corner of the cellar and, when the door was opened, snarled and tensed himself to leap at them. The soldiers had expected this. One had brought a cudgel along and when the dog began his forward spring as they ap-proached him, the man hit Boye a smashing blow to his chest. The poodle went down under this force, all the air in his lungs knocked out. Before he could get up to renew the attack, two troopers had flung themselves on top of him, holding him down while the third freed his chain from the post. The fourth Roundhead held a lantern so they could see to accomplish their captain's order.

The dog was dragged, struggling every inch of the way, by his chain up out of the cellar. Through the kitchens and down a long passageway they went, and as he went he dug frantically into the polished floors with his claws. His chest burned; he could not bark because of the tightness of his collar on his windpipe, but as he passed he snapped at everything in his way and hurled himself from side to side, trying to gain his freedom. By the time he had reached the square, dragged by three Roundheads, Boye's mouth was a mass of foam.

"He's gone mad!" shouted the blacksmith. "He's a mad dog!"

Addison laughed. "Nay, 'tis but the way of all Cavaliers —to act as if they had gone mad when their desires are thwarted," he told the smith. "The dog does not come willingly to his cage. He has made himself too warm. Parmenter, fetch a pail of water."

The trooper understood. He went to the nearby conduit and brought back a leather bucket of water while Boye, still resisting, was brought to the tail of the cart.

"Now!" commanded the captain. "Douse the cur! That should take some of the fight out of the demon. Then lift him into the cage, men. Do it swiftly!"

Parmenter threw the ice-cold water over Boye on command, drenching him from his muzzle to his tail. Blinded and shocked thoroughly by the suddenness and un-expectedness of this, the poodle put up no struggle as he was lifted and hastily shoved into the cage. A moment later the door was slammed shut behind him, and the blacksmith strode forward to attach the padlock to it.

"Now we have him fast!" Addison told the exhausted, swearing troopers. "When you go to the taverns this night, bid all of London come here to see Rupert's luck. 'Twill cost them not a farthing."

"Rupert's ill luck, he'll soon be, captain," a trooper prophesied.

The first night that Boye was caged was a wet, wild one. Cold winter rain poured down on him. Once he came forward to touch his nose to the bewildering bars. He pushed, then, against the door. He heard its hopeful creak and saw it open encouragingly for a half inch, but it would open no farther even when he threw his weight against it.

The poodle did not understand the cage; it was the strangest thing he had even known. He could see out of it on every side—even the top if he lifted his head—but he could not leave it. Finally in despair he went to one corner and crouched down on his belly, his head on his wet paws while he waited for dawn to come.

Within the first week of his captivity the Earl of Essex,

a man with unruly fair hair and heavy brows, came to see Prince Rupert's dog. He listened to Captain Addison's scheme to exhibit Boye, then nodded. "There is some merit in what you say," he told him. "It is no secret to me that the ignorant of my army call this animal a witch dog. Display him then, though I must tell you I do not truly like this." He turned away to enter his fine coach, followed by his officers.

One of the men who had come to the Roundhead troop's headquarters to view Boye with Essex stayed behind —even when Addison, too, had gone. He stood for long moments, gazing at the dog, who huddled shivering against the December cold. His face showed his disgust. Oliver Cromwell spoke to one of Addison's troopers. "See to it that this animal's cage is covered at night against the weather— if you fools would have him live!"

"Captain Addison gives orders here, sir," replied the trooper.

"Then fetch him down to me. Tell him Captain Cromwell would speak with him about this dog."

Josiah Addison heard the trooper's message out, swore, fastened on his sword again, and came clattering down to the square to see his fellow officer. "Damme," he told himself as he went. "This Cromwell stands high in the favor of Essex. I must listen to him if I want Essex's favor also."

That night a heavy weatherproof cloth was placed over the cage to keep out the wind and constant chill drizzle.

Chapter IX

Arbela Mary

THROUGH THAT long winter of 1642 and 1643, the Cavaliers and the Roundheads held off from engaging in major battles. They kept busy, however, preparing what to do in the spring, the best season for war.

King Charles at Oxford hoped to send his armies toward London to meet at the River Thames. If they took the bridges below the city, they could cut off Essex's supplies from the sea. If they also seized and held the bridges upriver from London, they could starve the city into surrender.

Rupert's work was to make safe the King's headquarters at Oxford. This meant he must drive off any Roundheads who pressed upon that town. Parliament's soldiers had garrisoned both Gloucester and Cirencester, dangerously near

Oxford. It was at Cirencester in January the Prince struck, riding with his troopers night and day under a fearful meteor-lighted sky. They failed in their attempt in January, but early in February Rupert's cavalry and foot soldiers won the town, taking many enemy prisoners.

Hugh Joliffe did not go to Cirencester with his master. He remained behind at Abingdon waiting to greet Rupert with joy when he returned. "Master," the page asked, as he served the Prince his supper, "where does the King next send you?"

"Who knows? Who knows?" The tall young man was morose. His shoulders sagged and his face grew mournful.

Hugh knew Rupert's thoughts from his expression. He had seen it often enough, hating it, for it meant the Prince thought of Boye.

"Has any word come here to you of Boye?" he asked the page.

"No, master," Hugh told him. This was true enough. Hugh expected no word. If Parmenter had killed the dog, it was not likely that the Roundhead would noise the word about so that the Cavaliers would hear of it.

In April Rupert rode to the north, to Birmingham, another enemy stronghold. This place his Cavaliers also took and later, according to Roundhead accounts, they murdered all the people and left the town in flames after they had drunk "health" after "health" in captured wine to Rupert's dog—"wherever he was." Their stories were not all true. Very few civilians were killed. Rupert fired only two houses to permit him to enter Birmingham, and but one sad "health" was drunk to Boye—"wherever he was!"

In May of 1643 the Prince went to Lichfield. Where he had taken Circencester and Birmingham easily, he found Lichfield a hard nut to crack. The enemy had taken up a very strong position in the old cathedral, and Rupert's light artillery could not smash its heavy walls. The Prince decided that he must besiege the town and hope to break into it or to starve it into submission.

Hugh came happily from Abingdon now with the baggage carts, which generally went where the great guns went. He lived in the camp with his master. Because Will Legge had been wounded and taken prisoner in a ditch before the town, and because Maurice was away, serving elsewhere in the royal army, Rupert was more often alone. He was closer to the page and spoke with him in the evenings.

"Will it be long before you take Lichfield?" asked the boy one night. He was more at ease now that there was no rival for Rupert's affection.

"Not long, lad. I shall have my sappers dig beneath the town. I do not like this tedious kind of war. I would rather lead my troopers at a gallop down a road into the enemy, but if I must mine under Lichfield, I shall do it." Rupert frowned. "I must make haste, Hugh. News has come from Oxford that the Earl of Essex lays siege to Reading where we keep a garrison. I am tied to the siege of Lichfield—the devil take this place when I would be at Reading if I could!"

Some few days later Rupert's tunnel was finished and quantities of gunpowder brought secretly into it. The Prince formally asked the Roundheads, who were unaware of his plan, to surrender. They would not. Then he ordered the charge of powder to be set off. It blew a great gap in their fortifications. Through it the Prince's men shot down the Roundheads who dared stand against them. Within a few hours Lichfield had fallen to the Cavaliers, and Rupert accepted the surrender of the enemy commander.

Hurriedly Rupert, leaving Cavaliers to hold Lichfield, took his troopers and his baggage wagons south to relieve the King's men at Reading. The garrison had been brought to bay and was in grave danger from the menacing Earl of Essex.

North of Reading the Prince found King Charles and his army. They joined forces and attacked, expecting the Cavalier garrison within the town to sally forth to aid them, but the garrison did not. The commanding officer in Reading didn't know the King and his nephew rode to their rescue. He had made a truce with Essex. When the other Cavaliers attacked the Roundheads stationed before the city, the Cavalier colonel was forced, by his word to Essex, not to help. The rescuing royal forces fell back and did not again attempt to take Reading. As for the colonel, he surrendered his sword to Essex.

The King's soldiers who had garrisoned Reading marched out through the gates. As they walked they were disgracefully attacked, hooted at, and robbed by the Round-head soldiers, who waited to move into the town and hold it for Parliament.

One of them, a young cornet—the officer who carried the standard—had been dragged away to the Roundhead tents by some troopers of Josiah Addison's command. Cornet Robins's boots were stout new ones, his cloak made of rich murrey-colored wool, and his breeches and coat of sky-blue satin. The Roundheads, Elnathan Parmenter among them, shared his magnificent clothing and gave him rags to wear.

Robins was roughly shoved about and ended on the ground half under a cart as his boots were pulled off by four Roundheads. Addison's troopers, soon tired of their play, left him alone hot with rage to don his rags. Few of them noticed how he got up and stood before the cart as he dressed himself in what they had thrown him.

The young Cavalier paid little heed to his robbers, but much attention to the cage the cart held among its barrels of provisions, pans and pots, and rolls of coverlets. He saw the large white dog lying on the cage's filthy bottom. Robins had never served under Prince Rupert, but he had been at Edgehill with King Charles's army and had distinguished himself by his bravery there, earning a word of approval from the King. He had marked out the dog the Prince had sent to the top of the hill with the King's two young sons.

He had once seen the poodle, too, at Rupert's Abingdon headquarters when he had ridden there from Oxford with several other officers.

His robbers were now fully occupied swaggering about in his clothing, calling for the admiration of the others. One of them, a long-nosed man with lank fair hair, was even using a lady's silver hand mirror to look at himself in his new murrey cloak.

The young Cavalier, a courageous man who knew little of caution, reached his hand into the cart, snapped his fingers, and whistled softly. When the prisoner-dog pricked up his ears, Robins whispered to him, "Boye! Boye!"

The white dog lifted his muzzle. His gaze was alert as he heard his name called—the first time in many months.

This was Boye Cornet Robins at once realized. He called out boldly to Parmenter, who now wore his cloak, " 'Tis Prince Rupert's dog you have here in a cage!"

The trooper came over to peer in pretended surprise at the poodle. "So it would seem," he remarked with a smile. "It does somewhat resemble the Devil's witch cur."

"The Prince has offered a reward for him," the cornet told the trooper.

"There's not that much gold in England. Essex holds Rupert's luck. The sight of this dog puts heart into the earl's men."

"You do a vile thing to the dog! See him. He's naught but bones and skin!" protested Robins.

"He can stand and snarl when he's poked with a stick,"

Parmenter told the cornet. "The witch dog has his uses. Now betake yourself to Oxford. Tell Rupert the Robber Essex has Reading fast—and his cur to boot. The dog goes into the town with us. If Rupert wants them, he must come take *both!*"

Robins took one last look at the wretched dog. At Parmenter's approach Boye had moved back against the bars, cowering as if he expected blows. "Aye, your message will be conveyed to the Prince though I walk the roads to Oxford with my feet bare—as you have left me."

"Be of good cheer that ye do not go to Oxford without clothing—as Rupert is said to have forced one of our officers to ride to Worcester after Powick Bridge!"

"Did you hear the Prince order this? Did you see this?"

"No," Parmenter told him, "but I believe it!"

"This dog was at Powick Bridge, I think," said the cornet.

Parmenter laughed. "He was, indeed!" He showed his scarred wrist to Robins. "I have this as a token of Rupert's cur. Tell your Prince this, too. Tell him not to send a ransom offer to me."

"I shall tell him."

Jeered at and in rags, the cornet left the Roundhead camp and rejoined the other members of Reading's garrison already on their way to Oxford. They could not go to the King and Rupert, for the enemy blocked their way and would not permit them passage.

An hour after the Cavalier garrison had gone, Captain Addison brought his men at Essex's command into the city. Parmenter, the driver, took his place on the seat of Boye's cart. Surrounded on all sides by rejoicing, shouting Round-heads, who no longer paid much attention to him, Boye entered Reading.

The months since he had been put into the cage had been terrible ones for the poodle. He had been fed and his cage covered against the weather in London, thanks to Oli-ver Cromwell's intervention, but he had suffered greatly. Many had come at first to see him. They had shouted at him and laughed at him. Some of the more cruel had thrown clods of dirt at him or had stabbed him with long sticks to make him disappear and, failing that, to move about. When he had been on view Boye had kept to the cage's center as long as there were no sticks in sight. This was because sol-diers would sometimes pinch him if he put his back, sides, or tail to the bars while they proved to themselves that this was a real dog, not a witch beast at all. When Roundheads brought sticks, he dodged them as best he could by moving swiftly about.

At night when he was finally left alone Boye paced. Instinct taught him that he should stay active. He walked back and forth inside the small enclosure for hours, but he never howled. Once when a full moon illumined his cage he had, and Parmenter had come out to prod him with a halberd, which had pierced one paw.

Wherever Addison's troop had ridden, the dog had gone in his cart. The Roundhead captain had detached Parmenter to haul the cage about and, when they encamped for a time, to spread the word where Rupert's witch cur could be seen.

Hundreds of soldiers had flocked to gape at Boye and to deafen him with their jeering. He had been displayed in county after county, town after town, and in all kinds of weather. By this time he paid little heed to the Roundheads who rode beside Parmenter's cart so long as they did not torment him. He braced himself against his bars in the jolting wagon and waited until Parmenter would bring it to a stop in Reading, only one town among many to the miserable dog.

Essex's billeting officers had chosen a particular inn to be Captain Addison's headquarters, the Rose. It was not the finest inn in the town, but then Captain Addison was not one of the most important of the earl's many officers. The inn, which was not far from the city gates, was a low building with a slate roof and many shuttered windows.

Addison did not fancy it. He guessed after one glance that other officers were better housed. When the plump, aproned host came fearfully out to greet him, with a pair of dark-haired children peering out from behind their father, the captain told him, "I'll require your stables and each and every of your rooms. Turn out your other guests. If you give me no trouble, I'll give ye none."

The frightened host bowed. "I am Peter Claycomb. All will be done to serve ye. I have no guests. King's men were recently quartered here. They are gone."

Addison snorted. "Scour out my room well then, I command you, if a Cavalier has slept in it. Take my horse now, Claycomb."

The landlord nodded to his lad, who ran to Addison's side, but the girl, an eleven-year-old, remained a few steps behind her father.

Arbela Mary watched, her hands folded under her long apron, as her muttering father hurried into the Rose to prepare "all" as he had done "all" for the Cavaliers who had left that day. She came forward slowly when Addison dismounted and her brother led his horse away. Arbela Mary had no interest in the horses the Roundhead cavalrymen rode. Her eyes were on the cart where she had spied out something very odd—black bars against the sky and the movement of something white behind them. The innkeeper's daughter had never seen such a cage before. What was it? she asked herself, as she edged toward the cart.

Parmenter watched the girl in the red-wool gown coming. It amused him to see children's faces when they first saw the dog he held captive. Their eyes grew very large and their jaws dropped, when he told them this was Rupert the Devil's witch dog. Most of them had heard of him and believed the tales told of the poodle's magical powers. Parmenter was pleased to tell them the truth.

"What do ye think I've got here in the cage?" he asked the girl. "A bear—a wolf?"

She shook her head. Arbela Mary was a shy child, who often dreamed when she should have been attending to the chores her father set her. "I don't know," she told him without looking at him.

Parmenter leaned over from his cart seat to speak to her alone. " 'Tis a dog. Come to the tail of the wagon and see."

Arbela Mary came slowly around the cart and peeked inside. "It is a dog!" she exclaimed, surprised.

"Aye, a dog in a cage—he is. But he's no common cur." The Roundhead laughed. " 'Tis Boye—Rupert the Robber's beast."

"Oh," remarked the girl. She added then, " 'Tis uncommon to see a dog in a cage."

"Uncommon, indeed," Parmenter agreed with her, "but this is a Cavalier animal."

"Is he?" she asked. She looked now at the Roundhead for the first time with narrowed green eyes. "The dog is very thin!"

"So he is!"

"What do ye give him?"

"Meat—meat and water, what did ye expect, girl—sweetmeats?"

Arbela Mary shook her head. "Do ye set him free sometimes?"

Parmenter shook his head now in turn. "The cur's never

to be set free. That's by orders of the captain. He has the key to the padlock—the only key there is. He keeps it in his pocket. Nay, the dog will not leave the cage until he dies in it—or until he's served his purpose. Then, I am to *shoot* him." He grinned down at the girl, hoping this statement would bring some response from her, but he was disappointed in her. She was not the sort to weep over the cur's plight.

The innkeeper's daughter's gaze flicked to the trooper and then back to the dog, who sat motionless in his cage. "He is a very fine dog," she said so softly that Parmenter could not hear her. Again she spoke up, "I have never had a dog. My father would not permit it, though we keep kitchen cats. Why not give him to me in place of shooting him?"

"No. Not even if I chose it. This animal is to die. I have my orders, mistress."

Arbela Mary gave Parmenter a strange little smile, one he did not understand, then turned away walking toward her father's inn. When she reached the stoop, she turned about and once more gazed at the cart, but this time not at the Roundhead but at the dog in the cage.

When she had left, Boye got up to stand against the bars, looking after her.

"I mislike it much," she said to herself. "A dog should not be kept in a cage."

Landlord Claycomb was a good host. He served roast

pig and plump swan to the captain. It seemed to the Round-head that the innkeeper's silent little dark-haired girl was ever at his elbow with another leather jack of excellent country ale. When Addison finally stumbled up to his chamber, the finest in the house, he was quite drunk. The landlord had to help him up the steps and out of his cloth-ing into his bedgown. Then Claycomb, who was very pleased at the orderliness of the Roundhead occupation of Reading, went downstairs to help his wife and the rest of his family serve Addison's troopers. He hoped they would not drink as much as their captain, although one of them, the long-nosed man who had driven the cart, was already asleep, snoring, half-drunk in the chimney seat.

Claycomb had not seen Arbela Mary follow him quietly up to Addison's room and halt outside the door in the black, narrow passageway. When he hastened down to the com-mon room again, he did not spy her out in the darkness. He did not know that she noiselessly opened Addison's door, made her way to the table, and found the captain's coat flung over a chair. While the captain slept, Arbela Mary put her trembling hand down into his pockets. In the left pocket she found what she sought—a large brass key, the only key he carried. She slipped it into her apron pocket and, unno-ticed as she had entered it, made her way out of the room.

For another quarter of an hour Arbela Mary with her brother and parents served the Roundheads. Then she told her brother, "I'll see to the captain's horse. Tell Father I'll not be long."

The innkeeper's son nodded. He had earlier seen to it that the mount had a manger of hay and oats and had been watered, but there was no doubt about it that the surly Roundhead captain was most particular about his horse. The Cavaliers who had been billeted at the Rose until that day had been easier folk to serve—though they drank every bit as much ale.

With a glance at the still snoring Parmenter the girl boldly left the inn by its front door, heedless of the other troopers' stares. They were comfortable enough. They would not care where she went. She let the latch fall and went out into the cool spring night. There stood the cage before the inn door, its bars a fretwork before the low-riding moon. The courtyard of the Rose, as Arbela Mary had known it would be, was deserted. All of Addison's troopers were inside where they could find food and ale and good service. Even the sentry, a man she'd carefully marked out before, had crept inside the kitchen for a tankard, telling the inn cook that Essex held Reading so firmly in his grasp that even a sentry could take a moment's ease. She had seen him there and had fetched out a bottle of good wine for him from her father's cellar an hour past. She waited on the stoop for a time, listening to the sounds inside the Rose, then came quickly to the cart.

Boye had heard the click of the door latch when the girl had come out. When she walked across the courtyard to him, he rose to his feet. The moonlight was bright enough for him to see that this person who approached him was no heavy-booted soldier. Still he moved warily away from her when she pulled herself up into the cart.

"Do not bark, white dog," she warned, as she took the key from her apron and fitted it to the padlock. "Do not bark!"

For a few moments Arbela Mary tried the lock, which was stiff with disuse and rust. Then it opened with a click. Carefully she moved the hasp away from the bars it held. The innkeeper's daughter next took a deep breath and opened the cage door. It creaked so much it made her heart pound. Then she fell back to one side of the cart for safety— now afraid of the big poodle.

"Go, dog!" she hissed at Boye. "Go!"

Boye knew these words as well as he knew "Boye comes," or "Boye, stay!" A gaunt, dingy shadow, he pushed his nose out of the door of his prison to make sure it was really open. A split second later the rest of his body fol-lowed. Then came the soft thud as he leaped out of the cart.

He was free.

Arbela Mary watched him disappear around the corner of the Rose out into the street, which led to the city gate. She approved of his caution—of how he moved swiftly from cover to cover. That is how she would do it if she had been the dog. When he was out of sight, she scrambled down out of the cart, shook out her skirts, arranged her apron and the scarlet ribbands in her hair, and marched across the court-yard to see to the captain's horse. She stopped for only a split second—to drop Addison's key into the dark water of the inn well.

Chapter X

The Wanderer

OTHER ROUNDHEADS had been quartered in houses on the street that Boye chose. Some of their baggage wagons were drawn up on each side before their buildings. The dog moved from the shelter of one cart to another, waited beneath it until he saw that the way was clear, then moved on. By fortunate chance he traveled toward the gate through which he'd entered.

Slowly, very slowly the poodle made his way to it, hiding himself behind anything he could find, barrels, high stoops, motionless coaches, and whatever else offered concealment. He had two narrow escapes. Once a woman came outside to throw a pail of supper scraps not far from where the dog hid. At that moment the moon lay behind a somber cloud so the housewife missed seeing him, only a foot from her doorstep. When she shut her door again, Boye crept forward to eat some of the scraps. In the excitement of taking Reading, Parmenter had neglected to feed his prisoner at all. Then Boye went on his way down the street until he was forced to leap for refuge behind a pile of timbers, avoiding three troopers who came plodding heavily toward him from the gate. They did not spy him out either.

For a time the poodle crouched in his hiding place, his eyes on the sentries at the torch-lighted gate. They walked back and forth, back and forth, first away from one another, then toward one another, meeting in the middle. The dog was frightened and confused by these men. He waited, tense.

All at once, startling him, someone in the house above him banged a shutter to. Boye shot out from behind the wood and at a terrified dead run passed between the Round-head sentries as they came toward each other.

He passed one soldier so closely that he nearly knocked the man to the ground. "What in the devil?" bellowed the sentry, raising his primed musket to shoot the animal that was bounding away, an excellent target, into the moonlit night.

The other Roundhead cried, "Nay, Giles, it was but a dog!" He had not recognized Boye, who had moved too swiftly for him to be marked as the famous witch dog.

Neither had the first sentry. He lowered the musket from his shoulder, laughing. "Perhaps 'twas a Cavalier beast

—going in haste to join the other devils on the road to Ox-ford," he said. "Yet perhaps it was but a very large hare we saw."

Boye ran as far as he could. Because of his months of imprisonment and scant food, it was not far, only about a half mile. But he was now in the countryside under the stars and at last free. Exhausted, the poodle crawled under a tall hedge and fell asleep in the warm night.

Early in the morning Elnathan Parmenter, who went outside to draw a dipper of water from the well, discovered the empty cage. He stared at its open door in disbelief, and then shouted for a trooper to "fetch the captain and make haste."

Some minutes later a yawning Addison came out of the Rose. His head ached; his hair was uncombed and his coat half-buttoned. "What d'ye want of me?" He was surlier than usual.

"The dog—the Devil's dog! He's gone!"

Now the captain awakened. His hand went to his pocket. It came forth empty. "My key! My key's been stolen!" he said as if he could not believe it. "Who would take it?"

"Cavaliers!" Parmenter told him.

"There are no Cavaliers in Reading, trooper."

"Then who would do this thing?"

At Parmenter's first shout Arbela Mary and her brother had come out into the innyard. The girl had never really intended to keep her secret. She did not fear the Round-heads half so much as her father and mother did. "I set the dog free!" she called out to the captain.

Addison swung about to gape at her. "Why did ye do that?"

"Because I *mislike* dogs in cages!"

The captain didn't know what to do. The girl's parents stood behind her, their faces fear-stricken as he glared at her. He was aware of how his troopers came tumbling out of the Rose also to gape at him, at the girl, and the open cage. He heard one of them mutter sleepily, "Do ye think the cap-tain'll shoot the little gel?"

This decided the embarrassed captain. He ordered some nearby troopers, "You—and you. *You there!*" picking out the man who'd spoken. "Search for the cur. Bring him back here. Parmenter, I will speak privately with ye." Care-fully the Roundhead officer averted his eyes from the girl, who stood her ground calmly—though her face was as pale now as her mother's.

Parmenter and Addison had words with each other on the other side of the cart. "Rid us of the cage," Addison told the trooper. "The dog has served his purpose. 'Tis of no importance now that he's gone. What the girl did is of no matter to me."

"What if the troopers you sent find the animal?" Par-menter's face was as sour as the taste of last night's wine in his mouth.

"We'll kill him."

"What of the lass?" asked the trooper.

"She shall be beaten with a stick. Her father will do it on my order if he is a wise man. The child is proud and willful."

"Shall I seek for the cur, too, captain?"

Addison shook his head. "I have other work for you."

"What if the dog makes his way to Rupert?"

The captain shrugged and said, "If the Prince has that serving lad still with him, the dog will find no warm welcome." He grinned. He lacked two teeth. "If you should see that lad again, what will you say to him, Parmenter? You were to have killed the animal."

The trooper did not meet his fellow Roundhead's eyes. "I do not expect to meet that lad again."

"I should think you would not choose to."

"But I tell you this, captain. I regret not keeping my promise to the lad now. If the cur crosses my path again, I will shoot him out of hand." He tapped his wrist. "I have not forgotten this."

"Aye, do as ye please, trooper. We will speak no more of the dog."

Parmenter watched his commanding officer go. He grinned when he saw him pause before the innkeeper to berate the man. When Arbela Mary's father caught her by the ear and dragged her off to the stable for her whipping, the trooper laughed.

* * *

Boye awoke at daybreak and crept out from under the hedge. He stood looking about him, facing west, the sun warm on his head and back. Parmenter had kept him shorn, although it had taken a clubbing each time and the help of four troopers to hold him down. He had been cruel with the shears, sometimes cutting the dog, accomplishing the task he hated, but the captain had ordered it, saying, "I have some little knowledge of this dog's breed. If he is not clipped, he'll seem more of a sheep than a dog. I'll not be mocked at for exhibiting a sheep that I claim is Rupert the Devil's witch dog."

Now the dog stood atop a hill. Below him lay a farm-house, an old building of gray stone. He sniffed the air. He scented the apple orchard in bloom behind the house and the sweet smell of burning wood. Hungry, but cautious, the poodle came out of the hedge's shelter and down onto the narrow path that led to the farm.

When he was halfway down it, a sandy-haired boy came from behind one of the farm outbuildings. He stood, his hand flung up to shield his eyes from the sun, and stared at the hillside. Then he whistled. The tune of this whistle made Boye stand motionless, although he had been at the point of running away. It held a note he recalled. He had not forgotten Rupert, but the memory of his master had dimmed during the terrible months the Roundheads held him. Now he heard this odd whistle a second time. Boye hesitated for only a moment longer, then came forward and at last stood trembling beside the boy who had, without guessing it, summoned him with Rupert's whistle.

The boy put his hand on the poodle's back and touched the sun-warmed fur. "What shall I call thee?" he asked.

The lad and his mother, a widow, had always stayed close to their Berkshire farm. They knew little of the civil war. Neither Roundheads nor Cavaliers had come to them to raid their dovecotes, hen roost, or small flock of sheep. They had never even heard of the renowned witch dog. They saw Boye only as a large stray white dog that had come, unbidden, to them out of the spring morning. They were not even knowledgeable enough to guess at his breed. They knew only that their old sheep dog had recently died and that perhaps this newcomer could take his place. So they fed him.

For a while they kept him, although the first time they put him among their sheep they learned he was no shepherd. He chased sheep until the bleating animals fell from exhaustion, but he didn't have the knack of herding them toward their pens. The boy would have kept the poodle as a pet, but his mother would not. No, if the dog could not earn his keep, he could not eat their food. Food was too hard won for that.

She forced her lad near nightfall one day to take Boye in their cart onto the road that led to Newbury and put him out at a crossroads.

Boye tried to jump back into the cart, but was driven

back by the lad, who stood in the roadside with tears rolling down his face, throwing clods of earth at the dog. When the dog sank to his belly, whining, the grieving farm boy leaped back into the cart, whipped up the old horse, and headed for home.

The poodle was alone once more. Bewildered, he watched the farm cart out of sight, then went to lie down beneath some bushes near one of the four converging roads. Before long a coach rattled by. It was not a market day at Newbury, so the roads were little traveled. This coach was the first vehicle Boye had seen. Unnoticed by its old coach-man or by its passenger, the poodle entered the lane it took and through the gathering dusk followed its wheels.

Reading was not besieged by Cavalier troops. From that town Prince Rupert rode away with his uncle to Oxford, less than thirty miles to the north. The little university city was ever loyal to King Charles, and at all costs it and the King's person must be kept safe when the Roundheads were at Reading, so near.

Cornet Robins, a footsore and extremely weary young man, came to the Prince's headquarters there. He stood before Rupert and bowed. "I was one of the garrison sent out from Reading, Your Highness," he told the brooding Prince, who sat on the edge of his bed while his handsome young page pulled off his boots.

"That was an ugly business," Rupert told him. "Your

colonel should not have made a truce with Essex. He cost us the town!"

Robins nodded. He had not approved of his colonel's action either.

"Have you something to tell me of events at Reading?"

Again Robins nodded. "Aye, Your Highness. 'Tis of your dog I would speak!"

"*What?*" exclaimed the Prince. "You have seen Boye?"

Hugh had caught the cornet's words, too, and gone gray with terror. He pulled off his master's boot so violently that Rupert fell back, clutching at the bed post, and Hugh went lunging halfway across the room.

"Your Highness, I believe it was your dog. The Roundheads have him—a troop of cavalry."

"Where? Where is he?" demanded the Prince.

"At Reading—in a cage!"

"*In a cage!*" Rupert thundered. "Boye in a cage?"

"Aye, they display him to Essex's army. One of the Roundheads who tended to him said that the sight of Rupert's luck put heart into Essex's soldiers."

"My God!" were the Prince's furious words. "How did the dog seem? Tell me. Are you certain 'twas Boye?"

"He came to me when I called him by name, Your Highness. He was gaunt but well enough, I think."

"Hugh," Rupert commanded the page, "tell my aide to come to me. I will send a ransom offer to Essex, himself, at Reading."

Hugh left, afraid to disobey his master, but he listened outside the door to the cornet's words. "It will not do, Your Highness. I was told by a Roundhead that there is not enough gold in England to ransom the witch cur. The dog bit this man at Powick Bridge. He has the keeping of him."

Rupert shook his head. "What does one Roundhead trooper matter? Essex's honor as a soldier should force him to send my dog to me. The earl has behaved well enough in the past. I thank you, Cornet Robin, for your news. It has been very welcome to me."

Soon Rupert's aide-de-camp, riding with a herald who bore a white banner, galloped to Reading.

There the Earl of Essex spoke with him briefly. Essex then sent for Captain Addison. He talked with him in private and finally came back to the Cavalier aide. "The animal was set free some days past," Essex told him. "A little tavern maid released him from his cage." The earl laughed. "It seems she mislikes dogs being locked up. I am informed that a scouting party went after the dog, but could not find him." The general now became very serious. "If the dog were here at Reading, I would send him with you now to the Prince. I'd take no ransom for him. This was never a business I liked. Convey my regrets to the Prince. War has its necessary evils!"

"Then the dog is lost?" asked the aide.

"It would seem so. If my men find the animal, I will have him sent to you, but I must tell you that he has been gone for some days, and there is scant hope of finding him."

The aide-de-camp bowed to the earl. Among twisted grins and curious glances from Roundhead soldiers, he and the herald, their flag of truce rippling in the wind behind them, left Reading to take their bad news to Rupert.

The Prince, who had had his hopes renewed, was plunged deeper into gloom when he heard his dog was lost. Even Will Legge's return to him when he escaped his captors for the second time did not much raise his spirits.

Hugh's feelings about Boye were mixed. A tide of anger had swept through him when he at first realized that Parmenter had lied to him and had not killed the Austrian cur. Then, when he thought Boye might come back, he had been seized with fright that the aide might be told of his role in the poodle's disappearance. But when the Cavaliers returned with Essex's simple story, Hugh was much relieved. He was enormously pleased that the dog was lost. What more could he ask? It was all he could do to keep from whistling and singing as he went about doing his chores for Rupert.

But his joy was short-lived, and he began to bite his nails once more. A few days after the Prince had received the news from Essex's camp, Rupert took to war again, making his renowned ride to Chalgrove Field. A Roundhead deserter in June, 1643, informed Rupert that a great sum of money, twenty-one thousand pounds in gold, came to Essex's headquarters—pay for the earl's soldiers. This money would be very welcome to the King's treasury, so the Prince was sent to take it. Seventeen hundred men rode out of Oxford with him.

Rupert took the Roundheads by complete surprise. The Cavaliers went silently through Chiselhampton and Stadhampton and galloped into Tetsworth at nightfall. They did not return the Roundhead fire when they were shot at. Speed was their chief aim, not a battle. All through that night they rode and at dawn they took the town of Chimnor and with it many Roundhead prisoners. Rupert could not find the enemy treasure wagons he sought, but on his homeward ride he did find battle again.

Essex's men had followed him when he left Chimnor, after abandoning his search for the Roundhead treasure. At Chalgrove Field four miles from Chiselhampton Rupert stopped, turned about, and faced the enemy he had cleverly drawn on. He stood his ground defiantly in a wheatfield. When it seemed he would be taken by a rush of Roundheads, he leaped his horse over a hedge into another group of the astonished enemy. Twenty of his troopers leaped with him. With their daring Prince they routed the enemy.

The Prince regathered his forces and with them charged. The Roundheads broke up into small parties and fled on their lathered mounts to shelter in nearby villages.

Easily Rupert won the day at Chalgrove Field and departed it. He retreated across the Thames from Chiselhampton, tranquilly riding through the town as he had ridden through it the day before.

He did not guess that Boye lay sleeping that night before the hearthfire of a fine country house only a half mile north of Chiselhampton.

The occupant of the coach that Boye had followed into the dusk some days before was named Lady Beaton. She was on her way home from Newbury where she had visited her great-niece. As she rode along she cursed the Roundheads, the chill spring night, and the deep ruts the farmer's heavy carts had made in the road. Because she was weary and because she was not poor, she stopped for the night at a country inn some miles from her house. There, when she got down from her coach to lean on her servant's arm and go inside, she spied Boye in the light of the lantern the innkeeper held.

"It is a *dog!*" the old woman exclaimed. "Where did he come from?"

"I do not know, my lady," said her manservant. "I have not seen him before."

"Nor I," said the mystified landlord.

"Stay, dog!" Lady Beaton commanded. Then she told her driver, "Take me to the dog, Andrew."

The command had been one Rupert had often used to

him. Boye knew it well. Although he trembled, he stayed
while the old woman came hobbling up to him. Her scent
was faintly familiar to him, dried rose petals and spices. He
had smelled it twice before, though he did not know it as
the potpourri used by both Susanne Marie von Kuffstein
and his master's youngest sister, Sophie. The poodle liked
this smell. He associated it with soft hands, loving words,
food, and warmth. When Lady Beaton tugged gently at his
collar, he followed her into the inn. There he accepted the
meat and meal porridge she ordered brought for him and,
when he had finished it, sat down before her, his eyes bright
on her old, wrinkled face.

Lady Beaton had once kept fine dogs, a pack of fox
hounds, until she had grown too old to hunt with them. She
knew dogs. Her gaze took in his size, the condition of his
coat, a short tangle of white curls now, and the keenness of
his black eyes. "I believe you are not an English dog. Once I
saw a dog very like you—in France it was. It was called by
a strange name I do remember." She laughed. "I know you
are not a common cur. How did you come here? I wonder.
Whose dog are you?" The old woman leaned forward in her
chair and called, "Come here, boy. Come here!"

Thinking she knew his name, Boye went to her immediately and put his nose into her hand, scenting her sweet
rose-petal smell. Then he permitted her to scratch him
under the chin, a thing that Lady Beaton, knowing dogs, did
well.

That night he slept beside her bed on the heavy traveling cloak her manservant spread on the bare floor of the inn
chamber for him. The next morning after a fine breakfast
Boye left with his new mistress, in the bottom of her coach,
keeping her company as the lonely old woman chattered to
him.

Boye spent six weeks in Lady Beaton's big quiet house.
He walked with her in her garden and sometimes went out
with her in her coach on pleasant days. She disliked nearby
Chiselhampton and would never go there. Instead, when
she had errands in town, she sent one of her four servants,
who adored her and were kind to the poodle because of
her.

One of them brought the news of the Chalgrove Field
battle to her. "The Devil Prince was but four miles from us.
He roundly whipped the Parliament men, my lady."

The old woman who sat in her garden, patting Boye,
only sniffed. "Soldiers! If one of them comes here to me, be
they King's men or Parliament's apes, I'll give him the rough
edge of my tongue if he tries to rob me!"

Six weeks after Boye had come to live at her house, the
eighty-year-old woman fell ill. The apothecary from Chiselhampton came to see her, then told her servants that she
had taken a chill from which such an old woman could not
hope to recover. Lady Beaton knew this well. She had not
required an apothecary to tell her she was dying. She called
her servants to her bedside. All were old, two nearly as old

as she. "I bequeath my house and lands to the four of you. My great-niece does not require these things," she told them dryly. "She is rich enough. The dog who came to me at the crossroads you will take to Oxford, Andrew. There you will set him down!"

"We will keep him with us, mistress," said her tearful maidservant, the youngest.

But the old woman shook her head on her pillow. "Nay, you must not! This is a house of old folk. My boy is strong and young. He must leave us!"

At the sound of his name Boye got to his feet from a rug at her bedside and stood where she could reach out and pull gently at one of his ears. "He is a fine dog. Many people would welcome such a dog! Remember well, friends. When I am dead, the dog is to be set free at Oxford." Lady Beaton smiled. "He does not know it, and he has made not one complaint, but with us he has been a prisoner."

Boye did not understand the death of his mistress. He had often seen dead men and horses on battlefields he had revisited with Rupert, but he had never known funerals. When Lady Beaton was borne away to be put into her family tomb in the nearby church, he was left behind, locked alone, in the large house. When her servants returned in their black mourning clothes, they heard his agonized howls.

"The white dog mourns our sweet mistress," said the

maidservant, who had a handkerchief to her nose, weep-
ing.

"Perhaps he howls only because he has been locked
inside and wishes to be in the garden," Andrew said. " 'Tis of
no matter. The dog goes to Oxford this very afternoon. Her
wishes will be obeyed, heaven rest her now. 'Tis but nine
miles from here to Oxford. I'll be home in good time for the
funeral feast."

"Aye, we'll all rest easier when we've done her will,"
said another servant.

Almost at once Boye was led by his collar out of the
room and put into the coach and the door shut against him.
Andrew took him northwest toward Oxford through the
drizzly summer afternoon, clucking to his horses to make
haste.

The poodle could not look out and did not know where
he journeyed. The leather curtains of Lady Beaton's coach
were fastened tight against him and the doors fast shut with
ropes to keep him in. He protested in a long series of yelps
and howls, but when they arrived in Oxford after a couple
of hours' journey the dog, worn out by his efforts to get out,
had fallen asleep.

The pealing of church bells awakened him at dusk.
Boye stood up in the coach, listening. They were vaguely
familiar to him. He did not recall, though, how he had entered Oxford with Rupert, victorious after the Battle of
Edgehill the year before, and how he had heard Oxford's

many bells then. He did not know that Rupert was in Oxford now. He did not know that his mortal enemy, Hugh
Joliffe, was with his master serving the Prince wine at the
very moment Lady Beaton's coach entered the town.

Boye was hauled down out of the coach in an alleyway
behind a row of tall old houses. Andrew did not want to be
seen. He was afraid someone might think he was stealing a
dog instead of disposing of one. "Off with ye, boy!" he told
the poodle not unkindly.

When Boye hesitated, Andrew threw a stone toward
him, carefully gauging it so he did not hit the dog. Boye saw
the threatening gesture. He heard the fall of the stone on
the cobbles far to his right, and fled down the alley out onto
a broader way. Escaping what he thought would be a
shower of stones, the poodle skidded around a corner and
came to a shivering, watchful stop before a doorway.

This was a tavern door. Oxford abounded with taverns.
A man had just come out of it and had stopped to gather his
cloak about him against the summer rain. He looked on,
astonished, as the white dog came charging into view.

"My God, 'tis Boye!" he shouted.

His sudden shout made the wary poodle swerve about
and run for safety, darting down another street. The trooper
did not follow him. Instead he plunged back into the tavern,
bellowing, "Major Legge! Major Legge!"

Chapter XI

The Return

CATCHING BOYE was no small problem. Cavaliers came tumbling out of the tavern at Will Legge's command, but in the maze of twisting streets the frightened dog was able to elude them by dashing down another lane.

At last Will gave up the chase and leaned, winded, against the side of a house. "The Prince must fetch him, himself," he told the trooper, who had come pounding along with him. "The dog will not come to my call—nor to yours. Go to the Prince. Tell him to meet me at the Golden Boar. We will seek Boye together."

The Prince was now with the King, not at his own headquarters. It was full dark before the trooper Will had sent was permitted to speak with him. No man disturbed the King when he took counsel with his soldier nephews, Rupert and Maurice.

The trooper came up to the princes at once when they had left the King and were in the royal antechamber at last. The man swept off his hat to them and bowed, "Your Royal Highnesses, I have news of the greatest import!"

Maurice laughed to hear this. He knew the man, a particular old crony of Major Legge's. "Will's got himself drunk and into a fight with one of the King's officers again, eh?"

"No." The Cavalier shook his head. " 'Tis news of your dog," he told Rupert. "He's here—in Oxford."

Rupert caught the man by the arm. "*You* saw him? You saw *Boye!*"

"Aye, Your Highness."

"Where is he now?"

Again the Cavalier trooper shook his head. "I don't know. Major Legge and I weren't able to catch him—no man was. The major sent me to tell you. He says the dog may come to *you*."

The Prince's face was alight with joy; then it sobered. "Maurice," he said, "I do not know what brings Boye here. Among the Roundheads he has suffered greatly—that we do know well. Perhaps he won't remember me. Perhaps he won't come to my call?"

The princes and the trooper rode to the Golden Boar and there found Will Legge and a half-dozen men of his command. Will wiped the ale foam from his mouth and with the others went out into the night. It had begun to rain, but that made no difference to the searchers.

"Take me where you saw him last," demanded Rupert.

"Aye, 'tis not far," said Will. "Take a lantern with you."

When they had arrived at the entrance of the maze of byways, Rupert walked forward alone, a lantern in his hand. He chose one turning and went down it, whistling. The troopers stayed at the beginning of the complex as Rupert had commanded them, ready to run to hold the animal if Boye came to him.

From where he crouched in the drizzle behind a barrel of reeking dried fish, Boye heard the familiar two-note whistle, the whistle the farm lad had used, the lad who had driven him off. No, he would not come forward to be betrayed again. Then, as he hid, he saw the tall figure of the Prince across from him where two narrow alleys intersected. The man, whoever he was, carried a lantern, which he held high above his head as he looked about. His plumed hat shadowed his face. He was wrapped in a cloak from his shoulders to the heels of his boots. Boye did not recognize his master. He knew only that the stranger was close and that the stranger sought him. Boye kept to his hiding place behind the barrel; his eyes followed the searcher as he walked away from him, still whistling. He saw the man shake his head sadly and turn to the right. Then from some distance he heard him take up the call in his deep voice, "Boye! Boye! Come, Boye!"

This brought the poodle to his feet. These words were

familiar. Lady Beaton had used them, and he had come to them. The baritone voice was haunting. The dog crept out from behind the fish barrel. Cautiously, keeping low, he left the alley and entered the lane where Rupert walked. He followed the tall stranger in the rain, the stranger who now alternatively whistled and called him. When the searcher with the lantern reached the turning, the man suddenly swung about and thrust the lantern as far above his head as he could.

Boye stood against the dark front of a house, his whole body tense as he watched the man who peered into the quickening storm. The dog sniffed for a scent, but because of the rain caught nothing. He heard the stranger's shout, "Boye! Boye!" In spite of his urge to flee again, the dog held his ground when the man came running toward him, splashing over the streaming cobblestones. An instinct more powerful than his urge for safety held him there, the rain half-blinding him, while the man put down the lantern and knelt in the filth of the Oxford alleyway to fold the trembling poodle in his arms. And then at last the dog caught it and joyfully recognized it, the scent of the man—Rupert's, his master's scent.

There Will Legge found them when Rupert had his voice to shout. The Prince and the dog had not moved, but by the lantern's light Will saw how the animal licked the man's cheek.

"I see you've found him," Will commented quietly.

"Aye," was the Prince's mumbled reply. "My 'luck' has returned." Boye's master raised his wet face to look at his friend.

"Come along, Your Highness," Will Legge told him. "It rains far too hard to bide here in an alley. 'Tis a mercy folk have not opened their shutters and pelted you with slops and the dregs of ale for all the noise you've made."

Beside his master at last in a dream of happiness Boye walked to Rupert's Oxford headquarters. All the way the Prince's hand rested on the dog's back or head. The terrible cage and the cruel Roundheads were far behind him now.

Rupert was pleased to see Boye in such excellent condition. The dog's weeks with Lady Beaton had brought him back to health; he was no longer so thin. The Prince's long legs took the stairs to his bedchamber three at a time, and the dog leaped them with him. Rupert flung open his door and shouted to Hugh, who had been brushing the Prince's renowned scarlet cloak, "See what I've found, Hugh. 'Tis Boye!"

The page dropped the cloak to the floor in his amazement. To disguise the look of fury he knew had crossed his face in spite of himself, he bent to retrieve it. When he straightened up, he had a glad smile for his master and a feigned glance of affection for the dog, but he did not come to them.

"Where did you find him, Your Highness?" he asked.

"In Oxford—here. God only knows how!"

"He is well, master?" the boy asked politely.

"Look at him. See for yourself! Come here. Greet Boye!"

Hugh walked slowly forward, his gaze on the dog, who at his approach stepped backwards away from him, his growl commencing.

"Boye!" Rupert chastised the poodle. The Prince tried to push the dog forward to the page, but Boye would not move an inch. Rupert sighed. "It is no great wonder, Joliffe. The Roundheads have mistreated him cruelly. He does not remember you. I had hoped this would not begin again!"

"I had hoped so, too, Your Highness," said Hugh, telling the truth he knew Rupert would not understand.

That night Boye slept at the foot of his master's great bed while Hugh lay awake not far away from them. On Rupert's orders, to give the dog a feeling of security and to let him know where he was, a long candle had been lighted, one to last the night. By its yellow light the envious page saw how the Prince's brown hand, whenever the man awakened, fell at once, fingers tangling in the sleeping dog's white mane of fur.

Alone much of the time because of Rupert's military maneuvers and his raiding for supplies, Hugh talked often to himself. Now he said softly, "I've done with Roundheads like Parmenter—liars and cheats. Now I'll work my own will with the Austrian cur. I'll rid myself of him with no man's help."

* * *

Knowing how the poodle felt about Hugh, Rupert kept them apart as much as possible in the months that followed Boye's return to him. When he raided Roundhead farms, he took the dog with him, fearing no great danger there. When he went to confer with King Charles, he left the dog in the care of either Will or Maurice, who had been almost as delighted as Rupert to see Boye once more.

Then very late in May, 1643, the Queen started on a journey to Oxford to join her husband. Henrietta Maria had come over from the Netherlands in a Dutch ship in March. She had brought ammunition, arms, and treasure with her. These as well as the Queen's person tempted the Round-heads, who came to attack her as she landed on the York-shire coast. Cavalier troops rode to her aid, two thousand of them, sent from York to escort her there. The Queen re-mained at Cavalier-held York for some months, but she yearned to be with the King again, so in May she decided to make the perilous southward journey through Roundhead-held country to join him. Five thousand foot soldiers went with her as well as fifteen hundred cavalrymen, six pieces of artillery, and two mortars. Still King Charles fretted over her safety. Essex and other Roundhead commanders were in her vicinity—though the redoubtable Oliver Cromwell, who was now a colonel, was still at Cambridge, where it was rumored he trained force after force of men.

Rupert was chosen by the King as the very Cavalier to protect Henrietta Maria on her southward march. He was

not to join his forces to hers but to keep his troopers between the Earl of Essex's army and the Queen at all times.

Because he would be in the saddle most of the time and
would have no real headquarters, Rupert left Hugh behind
in Oxford. Boye he dispatched to the King for safekeeping,
knowing that Charles would bring the dog with him when
he met the Queen.

Hugh sulked before the Prince left Oxford. Rupert
thought it was because the page did not go along with him
—not guessing at the truth that Joliffe resented bitterly the
poodle's being put out of his reach. Hugh now had poison,
the same poison used against rats in the ambassador's house
in Vienna. He had stolen it when an apothecary's back was
turned and the page was in his shop, examining his glass
bottles and jars. He had not yet had the opportunity to give
it to the dog without danger to himself.

Hugh, disappointed because he could not get at Boye,
got news of Rupert's many skirmishes with the Earl of
Essex. So did the young Prince of Wales, who had been
delighted to have the renowned Boye in his father's keeping,
though the dog paid less heed to him than he would have
chosen. He once told the poodle happily, "Would you believe it, dog? The Prince, your master, went out but half-
shaved to beat the enemy at Whitebridge. When he had
driven back the Roundheads, he returned to his tent and
shaved the other side of his face. I wonder what the Roundheads thought of that? 'Tis said he will meet my mother, the

Queen, at Stratford-on-Avon, and then we shall join them at Edgehill." The Prince's plump dark face sobered at the name of this place, then he patted the dog and sighed. "I think Edgehill will be a happier place this time, Boye."

Early in July Boye traveled with the King and the two young royal princes to Edgehill. Because Rupert had asked it as a favor, the dog rode in the coach with the King and his sons. Rupert feared the poodle would run away again. It never once occurred to him that Boye had not run away, but had been delivered by treachery to the enemy.

King Charles was not half as enchanted with the dog's presence in his coach as his sons were, but the little Princes demanded he honor Rupert's request. " 'Tis our cousin's dog —a worthy dog who was prisoner of the Earl of Essex—a prisoner in a cage, mind you, Father," exclaimed James. "He deserves a place of honor."

The King gave in to his children with a laugh. "Then it shall be as you wish, but he is to occupy a seat with one of you or the bottom of the coach. I will not be sat upon by a dog—not even by Rupert's luck, and when your mother has joined me, the dog shall join *Rupert*. Remember, this animal is his—not yours. And do not wheedle him to possess it. I forbid it." King Charles's face grew very somber now, and he clasped his white hands together. "I feared somewhat for Rupert when his dog was lost. He is a man of black melancholy and of dark thoughts. A pretty woman's face interests him little. Harshness is a large part of my nephew's nature.

The dog is more to him than just an animal. It has a meaning I do not comprehend. I know only that Rupert is now a happier man than he has been for some time. He is also easier to treat with in my councils." The King sighed. "At least as easy as I have ever seen him! How difficult it is to keep him at Oxford and not before the doorstep of London!"

At the foot of the slope of Edgehill the King halted his army to wait for Rupert and the Queen. The princes took Boye with them on an inspection of last year's battlefield. The dead had been buried and under the bright July sky the grass grew high and green, almost covering the signs of the battle. Young Charles turned over a rusted Roundhead helmet and showed it to James, who had been gathering pike heads in his hat. "Do you remember how we stood up there?" he asked his brother, pointing to the crest of the hill.

"Aye, Charles—with our cousin's dog." James turned his head to smile after Boye who was leaping across the field where the King, their father, had come so dangerously near to being captured by the Roundheads the chill autumn before. "Boye does not remember the battle or this place," the younger prince told his brother.

"Dogs are more fortunate than men and have far fewer enemies!" came from the older prince.

"What will happen when our mother comes?" asked James of Charles, who, in James's opinion, knew practically everything.

Already the older prince was a thinker, a lad who had seen much and who expected little. Charles shrugged, "I suppose we shall fight more battles. Perhaps we shall end the war soon—with one great victory, but I do not think we shall." He looked grimly at Boye, who had flushed a covey of grouse from the long grass. "Our cousin Rupert had the right of it when he went to London. We should have stood our ground and attacked at Turnham Green, but our father, thanks to his old advisors, would not!"

"Would *you* have done it, Charles, if you were king?"

"Aye, James. I trust Rupert. He will ever be my friend when I am king!"

Boye and Rupert had as joyful a meeting at Edgehill as the royal family did. The poodle came like a white thunder-bolt to knock the Prince down as he dismounted from his horse. James doubled over with laughter to see this. The little boy had missed his mother, but he found being embraced by her far less interesting than watching the tall, dignified Prince Rupert brought down by the onslaught of the huge dog.

"We have kept him well for you, Cousin Rupert," James told him, when Rupert had got to his feet again to fend off the leaping poodle.

"Aye, you have; you have, Your Highness."

"If Boye has puppies, may I have one?" asked the little prince. "Father says we cannot ask for the dog himself!"

Rupert smiled; so did the tiny Queen, who had over-heard the loud request. "If Boye sires a litter of puppies, you may have the best of all. 'Tis my promise." Then at the King's command, Rupert, with Boye at his side, went to speak with the King and to receive his congratulations on the victories he had won as he had escorted Henrietta Maria to Edgehill.

"James will not forget his request to you, nephew," the King told him jovially. "He will expect a puppy. So will Charles when he learns that you have granted one re-quest."

Rupert shook his head, "Your Majesty, I would not match Boye with aught but another *pudelhund*. And where would I find one in England who was half so fine?"

The joined armies moved on to Oxford unopposed and on their way met with excellent news—the news of the vic-tory of Roundway Down. Rupert was especially joyful, for this was his brother's victory. Maurice had left him to fol-low his own star and to serve as a platoon commander under another Cavalier officer. The Cavaliers had here destroyed the western army of the Roundheads. Essex and other com-manders, however, remained still in the field to be reckoned with.

Will Legge spoke of one of them to Rupert as they rode along. Boye was frolicking behind the Prince, now and then running back and forth to the call of Charles or James who, too, rode their mounts in the happy train. The King and Queen now occupied the coach.

"What have you heard since I have been gone?" asked Rupert.

Will replied, "Much of you, Your Highness. Somewhat of Essex and Fairfax and some interesting rumor of a certain Colonel Cromwell!"

"What of him? I do not know of him."

"It is said that he was at Edgehill when we gave battle to Essex. At Cambridge now Cromwell does what you have done—molds a force of men. 'Tis said that England—or for that matter, Europe—has never seen such a body of soldiers. Their discipline is iron, our spies from Cambridge tell us. This Cromwell is a man to be reckoned with, I think."

Rupert laughed sharply. "Who is he then?"

"A country gentleman from Huntingdonshire."

"And where has this country gentleman learned of war?"

Now Will laughed, too. "From books 'tis said. From books written about the campaigns of the King of Sweden!"

Rupert's horse shied as Boye came hurtling back along the line of mounted men to him. The Prince shifted uneasily in his saddle. "I like this not, Will, this clack of Cromwell. I do not think that a man who has had no taste of battle can learn overmuch from books, but this Cromwell has now seen battle and he reads of the King of Sweden, the great Gustavus Adolphus. No soldier was ever more able than Gustavus, I know. I have copied many of his tactics with my cavalry. Perhaps someday I shall have to reckon with this Oliver Cromwell."

Will nodded. "I think no two men in England will be more evenly matched, Your Highness. Where you are hot, Cromwell is cold. He is far more perilous to us than the Earl of Essex. His rise is swift among the Roundhead forces!"

The summer in Oxford was a merry one for Boye, but not for Hugh, who received his master happily and who disguised his hatred of Boye as cleverly as he could manage. Hugh, envious, had stood in the Cornmarket among the throngs who lined the streets of Oxford to welcome the Queen of England, who brought guns and ammunition to pursue the war. Rupert had not spied him out, but Hugh had spied Boye with the Prince, the dog trotting along happily.

After the battle of Edgehill the year before Oxford's welcome had been a remarkable one. This time it was frenetic. The insane shouting clamor of the crowd made Hugh nervous and made his head ache. Every bell in the city not melted down for cannon was ringing out, and every person in the old city cheered as the royal coach went by, Queen Henrietta Maria waving. Finally Hugh turned away in disgust to go back to Rupert's lodgings to await his master. Let the King take up his residence at Christ College and the Queen at Merton College. Only Hugh's position as page

to a prince mattered to him, that and Rupert's cur—and the
poison he had concealed in the bottom of his baggage.

The Queen's court ladies flocked to her at Oxford at
once. There Rupert, Boye, and Hugh made the acquaint'
ance of one of them, a dark-haired beauty, the Duchess of
Richmond. Rupert with his dog and his page sometimes
walked with her in the gardens of Merton College. The
duchess was a witty, clever woman, a great favorite of the
Queen's, and even younger than Rupert. For three days the
Prince attended her. Soon even the King wondered if Rupert
had fallen in love—but, no! The prince found her company
interesting and a contrast to his harsh soldier's life. Too, he
liked the way in which Boye took to her, but love her, no!

Boye had not forgotten Lady Beaton, who had been so
kind to him. He liked the company of ladies. He still associated silken skirts and perfume with kindness and excellent
food, and certainly the duchess did not neglect to feed him
well when his master brought him to her—although it was
usually marchpane candy he got, which Rupert found odd
fare for a dog.

On the day before Rupert took his leave to ride to besiege Bristol, a Roundhead-held port in western England,
the beautiful duchess spoke privately with him. She had
watched Hugh's face as he walked about the flower beds of
the college gardens with Boye on a leash. "The page does
not like your dog," she told the Prince, "and the dog does

not like him. I have seen his face when you show affection to the animal. The lad is very envious."

Rupert had laughed to hear this. "You are mistaken, Your Grace. The dog has simply forgotten Hugh. The page has been with me near as long as the dog. They will again become friends."

"No, they will not." The woman shook her head and reached down to pat the Queen's ugly, ancient lapdog, Mitte. "I think that that lad, if he got the opportunity, would put crooked pins in your dog's bread and butter." The duchess laughed at her own jest. "That is, if Rupert's luck will eat bread and butter? We will speak no more of this. I see that you will not believe me."

The Prince nodded. "Aye, Your Grace, I will hear no word against either of them—my 'luck' or my page!"

Both Boye and Joliffe went to Bristol with Rupert, Hugh, as always, with the baggage carts and Boye at the heels of Rupert's mount. Because the weather was July-fine, the dog did not have to spend much time with the page. Sourly Hugh cursed his ill luck as he sat in the cart atop bags of supplies watching the hated white dog frolicking about the Prince he so seldom saw.

Hugh liked best to be with his master in private lodgings, not on the march. There he had had Rupert to himself. For some wonderful months the page had basked in the Prince's affection—the months the Austrian cur had been held by the treacherous Roundhead. Hugh had brought his poison with him, but had no opportunity to use it, for on the march the dog was fed by Rupert or by one of his troopers. The page had now thought of putting poison in marchpane, knowing how the poodle liked and gulped down the sticky almond paste when the Duchess of Richmond fed him. In a town they passed through on their way to Bristol Hugh had bought some marchpane—supposedly for himself but in actuality for Boye. As yet, he'd found no chance to give it to him.

Maurice also rode to Bristol and there joined Rupert. The two princes stood on a hilltop and conferred about how best to take the port. Boye stood with them, happy at being reunited with Maurice. Then the Roundheads in Bristol suddenly became aware of the officers on the hillside and opened fire on them—cannon fire. The princes and the other Cavaliers hastily fled to safety.

This was the commencement of a duel between the great guns that lasted twenty-four hours. The sound hurt Boye's ears, but he did not howl or cower under the baggage cart. Instead he stayed by Rupert.

Unfortunately some of the Prince's soldiers attacked before he gave the order. Rupert was now caught short. He had to protect these men at all costs—this was his first duty. He had no time to command that Boye be tied in a safe place. "Boye comes," the Prince shouted to him, as he swung up into his saddle.

Boye came to war, sprinting beside his master. What a horrible scene lay before them. The Cavaliers who had attacked prematurely were being massacred. Their bleeding bodies filled the ditch below the city wall. The ladders other Cavaliers used were too short to scale the walls, and the heavy Roundhead fire cut them down as they tried to mount.

Rupert's infantry, which was being slaughtered, too, began to run away, and the Prince galloped to rally them. "At them! At them! For King Charles!" he shouted, as he dashed among them, his horse rearing. "Go with your colonel!" He had no time to look for Boye, who was almost beneath his master's horse a moment later when it was mortally wounded. A white flash, the poodle streaked to safety only in the nick of time as Rupert's horse screamed his death scream, reared again, and fell crashing to the ground.

Boye leaped to Rupert's side. The half-stunned Prince pulled himself to his feet by leaning on the great dog. Then both ran toward the Cavalier lines—Rupert to get another mount.

Soon they were back in the thick of the battle. Rupert now learned that the tide had changed in his favor. A daring Cavalier officer and his command mounted the wall and once inside had made a breach in it to let others enter. Rupert's men poured through. Before long the streets of Bristol were filled with fighting men, Roundheads and Cavaliers. All day the battle raged. Many Cavaliers, who had no cover while the enemy picked them off with musket fire from houses, died in the streets of the old port.

Rupert and Boye did not come into Bristol, but outside it the Prince and white dog were everywhere at once, it seemed to watchers. Rupert's chore was to keep the Roundhead forts outside the city too occupied to send forces inside it to aid their comrades. It was not until very late that July day that Rupert rode at last into Bristol to receive the surrender of the Roundhead commander.

The Roundheads were sent out of the city the next morning exactly as they had once sent the Cavaliers out of Reading. Now the same disgraceful thing occurred to the Roundheads as had occurred to the Reading Cavaliers. The Roundheads were set upon at the gates by a mob of the King's men, robbed and assaulted.

The news came to Rupert as he sat at breakfast in his headquarters, the house of the Lord Mayor. Hugh had just set a plate of smoking collops before him. Boye was at his side, his head on his master's knee, hopeful for some of the food from the Prince's plate.

"Damme," Rupert thundered, getting up. "I shall see to that. Fetch me my sword, Hugh." He spoke over his shoulder to his aide. "Get me a horse. I ride to the gate."

Prince Maurice sat across the table from him, waiting for his breakfast, too. With Rupert he ran to the stables, buckling on his sword.

Boye did not wait to be invited to come along. He dashed out of the door the princes had left open in their haste before the hopeful page could catch at his collar. Through the streets of Bristol he dashed, behind their horses. When they rode into the Cavalier mob with their naked swords in their hands to keep order, the dog was with them, barking and leaping. When the Roundheads had been rescued, Boye heard Rupert say sourly to his brother, "By God, Maurice, now I shall have to make apologies to the Roundhead commander for the conduct of these, my men. That is a thing I do not choose to do. What a rabble I command!"

Will Legge occupied the Lord Mayor's house with Rupert when the Prince was made Governor of Bristol by the King, who was delighted with his nephew's victory. The days in Bristol were joyous ones for Boye. He was ever with Will or his master, walking along the harbor, which lay in the center of the city, the bowsprits of ships protruding over the very streets. He loved the sharp salty air of the place and took delight in scattering the white gulls that strutted over Bristol's cobblestones. The Prince and the dog were soon familiar sights to the people.

Hugh kept much to the Lord Mayor's large house. The Lord Mayor, himself, had stayed on with his servants and his family, so many folk constantly surrounded the serving lad. Hugh chafed under this and looked on with fury when he saw Boye leave daily with Rupert while he stayed behind.

Hugh's semi-captivity did not last long. Rupert was too

valuable a commander to be kept long in one place. In late summer of 1643 the King sent him to Gloucester. Gloucester was a Roundhead stronghold, one blocking the road from the west to London. It must be taken if the Cavaliers were to take London.

The King had thought the Roundheads would deliver Gloucester up to him when he came against them with such a strong force of men as he had. He was very wrong. He and Rupert met with two of Gloucester's Roundhead leaders outside the town. Boye stood with the King and his master as they approached. He sniffed their musty scent, growled, and then began to bark—to bark as he always barked when they passed grainfields with scarecrows in them on the march. How like scarecrows these men were in their long black coats, white collars, and tall steeple hats. How badly they behaved to the King with scarcely a bow at all. How sharp their noses were and how short their hair.

Even the disappointed King had to laugh when one of them told him, "Sire, Gloucester among all English towns is most loyal to the Parliament. We shall not surrender it to you or to any man!"

"Indeed, not!" said the second Roundhead. "Indeed, not!" His gaze fell on the barking poodle, and he sniffed and wiped his nose on his coat sleeve. "Accursed witch cur," he remarked, turned on his heels, and left.

The King smiled down at Boye. "I think, Rupert," he told his nephew, "the Roundheads pay your dog more heed than they do me."

Rupert and the Cavaliers besieged Gloucester. To the Prince's joy the Earl of Essex, his chief enemy, came marching from London to its relief. This could mean battle. To Rupert's great anger, however, the King's advisors insisted that the Cavaliers permit Essex to enter Gloucester, and then try to cut him off when he attempted to return to London. Essex had few supplies and a large army. It would be easy, some Cavaliers thought, to starve the earl into submission.

Rupert, furious and nervous, scarce slept at all in the time when Essex marched toward Gloucester. Where would Essex's army be from day to day? What would he do? These were the questions Rupert asked himself and every other Cavalier officer. Essex was behaving in a most peculiar fashion. Uusually he was sluggish; this time, though, he moved swiftly. At Cirencester, south of Gloucester, the earl found forty Cavalier wagons laden with food. Essex's men, thanks to this windfall, did not starve now. With new heart in his army Essex gave order for his men to abandon the relief of Gloucester and return to London by the Newbury road. At his headquarters in Faringdon the Prince heard this news.

He knew it was up to his cavalry to block Essex's route to London. He must force the earl back until the King could bring up his foot soldiers to Newbury.

"Hugh," Rupert told his page, "we shall give battle. This is not to be a Powick Bridge or another Bristol where Boye was in danger. I must leave Boye with you. Secure him well in the wagon. I hold you responsible."

The page smiled at his master. "Aye, Your Highness, I shall tend to him well."

Rupert touched Boye's head, then Hugh's shoulder and turned away to fasten the ties of his cloak. He did not see the page take a twist of paper from his pocket, the paper that contained the marchpane.

"God bless you and be with you, master," Hugh told the Prince, as he rode out of Faringdon.

Some five minutes later Hugh Joliffe had molded the marchpane and some of the poison into a ball between his fingers. He crept along the bottom of the baggage wagon, his hand outstretched to the dog, the sweetmeat in the palm of his hand.

"Come, Boye! Come, Boye! 'Tis for you," he whispered.

Chapter XII

Marston Moor

PRINCE RUPERT did not choose to fight at Newbury. The country was an evil one for cavalry, composed of country lanes, hedgerows, and fenced ground. How, he asked himself, could he charge here? He knew that this victory, if such there was to be, would be won by foot soldiers.

Nevertheless, Rupert attacked the Roundhead rearguard not far from Faringdon and pushed the enemy back into Hungerford that night. His work was for a time accomplished. King Charles had had time to take his foot soldiers into Newbury.

The King now held Newbury; Rupert and his men drew up forces on the south of the town, the Prince almost for the first time hoping he would not be required to give battle. Fate forced his hand.

The Roundheads occupied a hill that dominated the whole Cavalier line, a hill the King's officers had stupidly overlooked the night before. When they awoke, they found the hill blocking their path and alive with heavily armed Roundhead infantry. The Cavaliers charged it with troopers —not Rupert's force, but that of another officer. These unfortunate men were driven back by the enemy cavalry and massacred by Roundhead musketeers hidden among the wooded lanes.

Rupert, himself, chose more wisely—the only open ground near Newbury. As always, he preferred speed to safety. At his command his officers removed their heavy helmets, breastplates, and coats. They rode like their leader in their shirts, their swords in their hands. The fury of their onslaught forced the Roundhead cavalry to flee before them.

Captain Addison had come to Newbury with his troop. He and most of his men had survived the Cavalier attack on the hill, the attack in which Rupert did not take part. This second time Addison was not so fortunate, though. The wild charge of the Prince's troopers broke Addison's courage. He turned his horse's head to run before Rupert the Devil and the line of Cavaliers who swept forward across the entire open field, but before Addison could get away the Cavaliers were upon him with their swords. He screamed as he went down under a white-shirted trooper's slashing cut through his arm and shoulder. Then, mortally wounded, doubled over his horse, the Roundhead captain left the field to bleed to death among the hedgerows.

Elnathan Parmenter, who had been riding two ranks behind him, saw what happened. He spurred his horse toward the man who had cut down his captain and fired his pistol at him. The Cavalier, a young man with long russet-colored hair, fell from his mount, dead. Then Parmenter turned his attention to Rupert. There was no mistaking the Prince. He wore his scarlet cloak and he was alone, his horse prancing, in the middle of the field looking about him, shouting encouragement.

Parmenter galloped toward him, his sword ready. There was no time to stop to reload his pistol, so he would kill Rupert the Devil with naked steel. But this was not to be. As Parmenter's mount rushed forward he stepped into a fox's hole, and the Roundhead was pitched over the horse's head onto his face. There he lay, unconscious, while the Prince rallied his cavalry and led them again and again into the pikes of the Roundhead foot soldiers, soldiers who retreated step by step until they found the shelter of the hedgerows.

At dark the battle of Newbury ended. The lines of infantry kept their places and that night slept on the grass, expecting battle again the next day.

When it was full dark, Parmenter, who to save himself had pretended to be dead—only another dead Roundhead trooper in the grass—got to his hands and knees, and crept across the field to where he knew Essex's foot soldiers had retreated. He knew which direction to go. Rupert, himself, had told him, looming above him at sunset speaking with Will Legge. The Prince had not seen Parmenter's body jerk with fear when they reined in their mounts only a foot or so from him.

"The cursed Roundheads flee to the hedges," the Prince had complained to Will. "What vile country for mounted men."

"Aye," Major Legge, who had much distinguished himself by his bravery that day, agreed. "Vile indeed, but I think the day is ours."

"Is it?" snorted Rupert. "The King sends me a message. He will draw back to Newbury. He does not have gunpowder enough to fight tomorrow."

"Damme," Legge cursed. "Will nothing ever go aright for us, Your Highness?"

"It does not seem so," agreed the Prince. "My men are weary; their mounts are exhausted. Never would I have believed Roundhead rabble from London could stand so well against us. I do not think the King will have the wit or wisdom to pursue them. That is because his advisors lack boldness—the Earl of Bristol and the lot, curse them. They are costing us the war. It will be won by a man of boldness, one who is given a free hand, the free hand I should once have had to march on London. Come, Will, the day is past.

A poor victory it has been for me!" With these words the Prince rode away toward Newbury and the royal camp.

Trooper Parmenter made it safely under cover of the moonless night to the other Roundheads and gave them the watchword of the day. He lay that night, wrapped in a borrowed coverlet, thinking about Rupert who had been within pistol shot but who had yet ridden away. The Roundhead did not think now of the Prince's dog. Since the innkeeper's daughter had set the witch cur free at Reading, not one word of its whereabouts had come to him. He thought Boye to be lost. All the same he had not forgotten his promise to himself.

As he ate a scant cold supper given him by a Round-head foot soldier he mumbled to himself, "I did not kill the dog. I did not kill Rupert. Perhaps I'll have a third chance. Luck comes in threes!"

Boye watched Hugh come wriggling toward him with the marchpane in his hand. The dog's hackles arose as he backed away into the cart's corner. No, he would not take something from this person who hated him and whom he hated. He scented the sweetmeat not the poison, for it was nearly odorless and the heavy scent of the almond paste covered it. Although he loved this candy, he would not come forward to snatch it off the boy's palm. The poodle would take nothing from Hugh—nothing from his hand.

Food the page put down in a bowl or a bone flung to him Boye would eat, after Hugh had retreated to the proper distance—but take food from the serving lad's fear-stinking hand, no.

As Joliffe came ever nearer with his deadly offering, the dog, who was tied to one of the wagon's posts, began to snarl and to show his teeth.

Hugh realized that the rope gave the poodle room to attack him if he came any nearer, so he remained just out of reach, wheedling. Yet Boye would not come. At last in a rage of disappointment the serving lad threw the sweetmeat over the cart's tail, got out, and ground the marchpane under his heel.

The page folded his arms and leaned against the side of the cart. It was clear to him that the Austrian cur would not be fed poison in candy, although there was nothing he fancied more. It would be too risky for him to attempt to poison Boye's meat when so many folk were about. Hugh bit at a hangnail and thought. He could not shoot the dog. Then, as he pondered, a trooper came jogging along on a wounded horse, looking for a remount. The page saw the blood on the horse's flank.

He nodded. Aye. Now he had the right of it. Round-heads could not be trusted to do as they promised. Dogs did not always gulp down what they should. Battles, however, harmed animals as well as men. Witness the trooper's bleeding horse!

*   *   *

After the Battle of Newbury Prince Rupert went to Wales as its President. Boye adored winter there—he and his master were alone in the wild, wooded country. Maurice had fallen very seriously ill at Exeter, and Rupert had dispatched an unwilling Hugh Joliffe to nurse him. Hugh had not wanted to go with the Oxford physicians Rupert had also sent to Maurice, but he had no choice. He dared not disobey his master, so he rode away with the physicians in their coach with a long backward glance of malice at the white dog, who went to Wales when he could not.

For a retrieving dog Wales was exciting, filled with streams and forested hills. Sometimes on clear days Boye hunted with Rupert across the snowy fields. The poodle appreciated snow as much as he liked the wild storms that swept across the countryside and forced Rupert to stay quiet beside the hearthfire, where the dog lay at his feet, contentedly watching the flames.

Rupert's work lay in arranging his uncle's affairs in this loyal part of his kingdom and in writing to Cavaliers in Ireland asking them to send over Irish soldiers for the King. He knew that members of the King's council at Oxford worked always against him, and he found life confining in Wales when he received Will Legge's messages of how badly things fared.

Boye's days of joy came to an end ere long as they always had done in England. Rupert was ordered to Shrewsbury early in February of the new year, 1644. The situation was now a very difficult one for the Cavaliers. The town of

Newark, north of Oxford, was under siege by the Round-heads. Newark was important because, held by the Cava-liers, it lay in the center of a strip of land controlled by Roundheads. This strip of land split Cavalier England into two parts. Who held Newark held a very important posi-tion.

Hugh had come to Shrewsbury from Maurice's bedside with the happy news that Maurice mended quickly from his fever. At Shrewsbury he remained behind complaining when his master rode to the north, taking Boye and Will with him. Again Rupert planned to move swiftly and travel light.

"I want to go," grumbled the page. "I can ride a horse as well as any man. I am as tall as many troopers now."

"And but fourteen years old!" the Prince told him. "You could not spend day and night in the saddle as we do."

"Why does the *dog* go with you then?" demanded Hugh Joliffe.

"Because he does not put me to the trouble you would. Now, let us hear no more about it. You are comfortable enough here at Shrewsbury, I think!"

Will was in the chamber, too, while Hugh readied his master's clothing for the journey to Newark. Not usually a perceptive man, Legge nonetheless noticed how sulky the page was and, too, saw his black looks at the dog. Will guessed at the lad's envy, but said nothing to Rupert about it as they rode out of Shrewsbury with Boye frisking at the side of the Prince's horse.

Far ahead of his foot soldiers and great guns, Rupert came to Newark. By the light of a full moon the Prince circled the town and took up a position on a hill from which he could look down into it. The Roundheads were strong in that strip of countryside, very strong, and the Cavalier garrison in Newark was half-starved by now. The Prince's forces were fewer than those of the besieging enemy and his infantry and guns had not yet caught up to him. Still he decided to charge the Roundhead cavalry.

First of all, though, he sent Will, whom the poodle would obey, to lock Boye up in the one room of a small stone farmhouse. Will accomplished his task with difficulty. Boye guessed from the air of excitement about the troopers and the restlessness of their horses, which had also caught the tension, that there was to be a battle. He chose to be part of it.

As Will rode away he heard the dog's yelps of resentment at being left behind in the cottage, whose owners lay in the loft above, shivering in fear. Laughing, he told the Prince of the poodle's behavior. "Boye will wake the dead in the churchyard nearby with his infernal noise," said the major.

"Better he do that than be killed today!" the Prince replied grimly. "I have never seen so many Roundheads before. They grow stronger and more able each time we give battle to them, Will."

"The best soldiers of all, Cromwell's men, are not here. Perhaps we should give thanks for that," commented Legge.

"Cromwell won at Winceby against Cavaliers not long after the Battle of Newbury. Bear that in mind, Rupert."

"I also bear in mind that he is well enough thought of to have been made a lieutenant general by the Parliament," Rupert added. " 'Tis intelligence I received but three days ago. Aye, Will, I am not at all unhappy that Cromwell is not here today. I have the premonition that we shall win this day, but our task will be no easy one."

Nor was it easy. When some weeks later Hugh Joliffe heard of his master's relief of Newark, he grew white with fear. Rupert, who had never yet been touched by a bullet or by a sword, though Maurice and Will Legge had taken several wounds by now, had been in mortal danger at Newark. Three Roundhead troopers had come riding down on him at once. One of them the Prince killed with his sword and sent falling headlong to the ground. The Prince's aide shot the second Roundhead to death as he took aim at Rupert, but the third closed in near enough to grab the Prince by his collar and pull him from his horse. Only the quick action of one of Rupert's Irish officers saved him. The Irishman came thundering by at a gallop and with a blow of his sword cut the Roundhead's hand off at the wrist, forcing him to gallop from the field, trying to stop the flow of blood with his remaining hand. After this, the Prince's troopers charged and sent the enemy before them, driving them into a hopeless position. Rupert held the only bridge across the river, cutting off the retreat of the Roundheads. Also, his foot soldiers and his cannon had begun to arrive. Wisely the Roundheads surrendered.

The victory was not a great one, though it delighted the King and his court at Oxford. Rupert, disappointed and angry as usual, spoke of it to Will when they went back to the cottage to retrieve Boye.

"I have no army to follow up my victory. I have too few men with me. Damme all, Will! What I should do is attack the enemy and attack again and drive them into the sea. But I cannot. I never have enough. I must go back to Wales and try to recruit more soldiers. This is not the war I choose to fight!"

"Aye," Legge told him. "Shall I come to Wales with you?"

"No, Will. Send me letters from Oxford. Let me know what is going on there behind my back!"

"I shall," Legge promised, then he added. "Let the page stay with me—or let Boye remain at Oxford to keep me company."

Rupert turned to Will, astonished at the request. "I had thought to take them both to Wales. Maurice is well enough now; he does not require Hugh's services."

"Rupert, the page mislikes Boye."

"I know that. 'Tis the fault of the dog. Boye has never loved Hugh—though the lad has done him no harm. Since Boye has been with the Roundheads, his temper is less friendly, but I do not wonder at that. He was basely treated. I do not understand why he hates the lad who serves me. It is some fancy of Boye's—some whim. My dog and my page are both dear to me."

"Then keep them apart—or send the page away!" warned the major.

"Very well, I will keep them apart, as much as I can. Will, you keep the lad with you at Oxford. Set him to his lessons. He cannot accompt well. Boye goes with me to Wales. If I must choose between the two of them, I will chose Boye. He was with me before Hugh came to me. But I cannot dismiss the orphan lad."

Hugh's life serving Will did not suit him at all. Will was but a major, where Rupert was a general. Will was a common man, Rupert was a prince. With Legge in his hum- ble lodgings Hugh was more sulky than ever. He fought with the apprentices in Oxford, picking quarrels with them, and he greatly disliked walking about the town following the plainly dressed major. The two miserable months he spent with Will told on his temper. He was in an ugly mood when Rupert and Boye returned to Oxford late in April.

"I will go with you *wherever* you march this time," Hugh burst out to his master. "If you do not take me, I shall run away!"

Rupert laughed at this piece of boldness. "I do not know where I shall go next, lad."

Hugh put in stubbornly now, "I don't care, Your High-ness. I wish to go." He pointed to Boye. "The *dog* goes! He *always* goes! Why can't I go?"

The Prince gave in with a smile. "I promise that I shall take you along the next time I take baggage wagons with me."

The Prince had consulted once more with King Charles and his advisors and from them learned what he had ex-pected—that the Scots had decided to throw in with the Roundhead armies and stand against the King. The northern forces of the Cavaliers were preparing to fight against the Scots who advanced on them. The King's commander at York had readied himself to be put under siege—both from Scots and from Roundheads, who now marched northward to join them.

As he had relieved Newark's siege, Rupert was com-manded to relieve York's. He left his headquarters on the sixteenth of May with an army of two thousand cavalrymen and six thousand foot soldiers. On the way he hoped to collect more loyal troopers.

With him went both his page and his dog—Hugh with the baggage train, Boye trotting happily beside the Prince, enjoying the May breezes, which bore the scent of fox and hare to his eager nose.

Sometimes he ran off to flush birds in nearby fields, hoping that his master would come behind him with a fowling piece, but Rupert did not. Instead he whistled to the dog, and the poodle came, leaping hedges and ditches to his side.

The Prince took the town of Stockport nine days after he had left for York on his roundabout course. Three days after that he came to the defense of Lathom House where a brave noblewoman, loyal to King Charles, had held out with her tiny garrison against besieging Roundheads. Rupert drove off the Roundheads for her, and rescued the countess, who came to greet and thank him. She accepted the flags of the defeated Roundheads, who had with their mortars shattered parts of her fine home. The courageous lady smiled at the Prince and at his large dog.

"I thank you, Your Highness," she told the young man. "I could not have stood much longer against the enemy."

"I thank you, my lady," Rupert told her. "I thank you for your loyalty to the King's cause in holding out as long as you have done."

The countess looked at Boye. "I had hoped you would come and would bring Rupert's luck with you. I have heard much of your dog, Your Highness."

"He is, indeed, my 'luck.' I do not know what I would do without him."

Her face, which had been merry, grew sober. "You ride now to the relief of York?"

"Aye, my lady."

"Then wear my token there." The countess took a green

ribbon from the front of her dress and gave it to the Prince.

"I have worn no lady's favor before, but I will wear yours," Rupert told her with a bow.

"I have heard that you look with favor on no particular lady. I am wed, the mother of nine children, and quite old enough to be *your* mother. Say to yourself when you wear my ribbon that 'tis a token from your mother, too."

Rupert's smile was twisted. "I shall say to myself, my lady, that it is a token from the brave defender of Lathom House."

From Lathom House the Prince took his Cavaliers to Wigan, where he found the streets bestrewn with flowers to greet him. Boye was pelted with blossoms and greatly amused Rupert when he tried to shelter himself behind the Prince's horse to escape the shower of roses.

At Liverpool, a Roundhead town, Rupert was not so cordially received. He knew he must take the port because it was here he hoped reinforcements from Ireland would land to support the King. To enter it he was forced to bring up his artillery and shoot openings into the mud walls. When he did get inside he found few Roundheads remained behind. Most had fled him by sea. A few were taken prisoner. These Rupert questioned carefully before he set out for York.

From one prisoner he heard what he had long expected to hear someday. "The Earl of Essex does not march to York. Cromwell and others are in York now."

"What is the size of your army there?" demanded Rupert.

Terrified of the Prince, the Roundhead prisoner blurted out, "Over twenty thousand men!" His words, in spite of his fear, were proud ones, for he knew that Rupert had far fewer.

Hugh knew it, too. He stood behind his master's chair listening to the prisoners as they were brought in, one by one, to be questioned. He knew that in all the Prince had but thirteen thousand horse and foot, and little hope of more joining him before he attacked the enemy at York. The page's hands whitened on the back of his master's chair. What would happen to him if Rupert were killed? Where could he go? He looked at Boye, who lay at the Prince's feet, and thought about the dog. Any trooper in the army would want to own the poodle, the Prince's famous dog, but who would look after him? Maurice was gone, serving under another Cavalier officer. Will Legge was also gone, serving as Rupert's appointed Governor of Chester. Either of these would be proud to fall heir to Boye, but what of him, Hugh Joliffe?

The Prince and his baggage train soon left Liverpool and marched north and east toward York. There was a peculiar restlessness in the air of Rupert's camp each night. The page felt it; Rupert was often deep sunk in thought and talked to himself long after he had conferred with his men.

The dog caught this strange fever and rested along the

march as little as his master. He often got down from Rupert's bed of his own accord to lie on the floor, because the
Prince tossed about so. There the dog lay, as far as he could
get from Hugh's bed, listening to the Prince's mutterings
and the lad's restless thrashing about.

The Roundheads soon learned of Rupert's approach to
relieve the Cavaliers at York. They consulted one another
and made their decision. When their scouts told them the
Prince with his thirteen thousand had reached Knaresbor-
ough, seventeen miles across country from York, they quit
their siege of the town and moved out onto Marston Moor, a
field which lay in Rupert's line of march.

Rupert's scouts were as excellent as the Roundheads'.
They brought him this bit of intelligence, and he moved
swiftly—to the north. He came to York on the first of July.

Alone, his officers bidden to stay away until he called
them, the Prince sat his horse on a little rise. He looked
down at the poodle, who sat now beside him, gazing up at
his master as he spoke to him. "Now, Boye, I could refuse to
give the enemy battle, take the Cavalier garrison out of
York, and then march away in any direction I choose. I *shall*
give battle here. I have a letter sent me from the King. He
commands me to fight!" Rupert's face was long. "We are
badly outnumbered, my lad, but I will give the command to
move on Marston Moor where the Roundheads await me.
Then I must deliver you to Hugh at the carts."

The Prince rode down the hill, gave the order to his

aide-de-camp and officers, and then cantered back to the baggage wagon, on the way receiving the cheers of the troopers and foot soldiers. "Hurrah for Rupert and for Rupert's luck!" some of them shouted, as the man and the white dog went by.

Hugh sat dejectedly in the back of the cart, but his face brightened at the welcome sight of his master. "We go to Marston Moor now, Hugh. My troopers all wear green sashes today. You wear one too. Keep my dog safe. If aught should happen to me, guard yourself and Boye well. He is to be my brother's then. Do you understand?"

Hugh burst into tears, "What of me, master?"

"Take service with Will Legge again—you are near grown. No, better yet, choose your own master. Now I shall tether Boye well."

Rupert swung down from his saddle, took the leather rope he always carried in his deep coat pocket, and fastened it to Boye's collar. He clasped the dog in his arms but once, and then called for his scarlet cloak. For the unhappy Hugh he had one squeeze of the shoulder, no more, and the final words, "Take care, Hugh, that I find you both well on my return!"

Rupert mounted again and cantered away. Hugh, who sat beside the captive dog, did not see the Prince rein in his horse to speak for a moment in the dusty road with one of the wagon drivers, a grizzled old man in a black coat. "Take your wagon back to where you'll find my page and my dog," he ordered. "Watch them both for me well, and I'll reward you."

The old man took his long clay pipe from his mouth before he answered, "Aye, Your Highness, I'll do it. Do we give the Roundheads a fight today?"

"We do—at Marston Moor!"

"God be with ye, Your Highness!"

"Thank you," the Prince told him gravely.

When the famed scarlet cloak was no longer in sight, thanks to the summer dust, the carter drew his cart off into a field to watch the baggage train go by until the Prince's personal baggage wagon would catch up with him. For some twenty minutes the old man waited until he spied the cart with the tearful lad sitting in it and the shape of the white dog tied in its rear. Then he brought his cart beside the Prince's on the narrow road to Marston Moor.

Although the Earl of Essex was not at Marston Moor, Elnathan Parmenter was. He had never been popular in Captain Addison's troop. After the captain's death at New-bury, he had asked to be transferred. Parmenter had heard much of Cromwell's fine army. He rode to it when Essex let him go, offering his services to one of Cromwell's junior officers, who gladly accepted such an experienced trooper into his cavalry. Parmenter had ridden in this company for three months now. With Cromwell he had besieged York and fallen back on Marston Moor.

Like other Roundheads, Parmenter had not at first believed that Rupert would offer a battle at all to them. The
Roundheads had retreated to the south, expecting nothing
that day, but when a messenger came galloping, shouting
the words, "Rupert comes! The Devil comes!" Parmenter
had turned with the rest and gone to meet the Cavaliers.

Near nightfall the two armies were drawn up facing
one another. Rupert had received some reinforcements, but
still had but seventeen thousand men to the Roundhead
twenty-seven thousand. The Prince stationed his forces on
the north side of a shallow ditch, a ditch he lined with his
musketeers. With Rupert were two other Cavalier officers
and their men. On the opposite side of the ditch lay the
Roundheads under five of their ablest leaders. Oliver Cromwell's force directly opposed Rupert's on the west side of the
moor, less than five hundred yards from one another.

It would be an ugly night. Already the sky was heavy
with gathering clouds. The wide green shoulder sashes the
Cavaliers wore took on a strange grayish-yellow shade in
the murk of the approaching storm.

The Prince looked up at the blackening sky. Then he
stood up in his horse's stirrups and cried out to his Cavaliers
behind him, "Is Cromwell now there? Does any man know?"

An officer came trotting his mount over to the Prince
and told him, "Aye, Your Highness. Men have marked him
out. He is there commanding the cavalry directly before
you!"

"Then we shall attack on the morrow—in the morning. The night will not favor us," said Rupert. "Give the order."

The Prince left his horse in the care of a trooper and went to sit on the grass not far away. He called for food. Cold meat was brought to him. Other officers came to keep him company. Some of them had been at Powick Bridge.

"Do you remember, Your Highness, how we sat on the grass outside Worcester one day?" one of them asked.

"Aye," replied the Prince. "That was the day we won our first victory—the day of Powick Bridge!"

"The day your Boye was with us," said another. "The men miss Rupert's luck tonight."

Rupert sighed. "At Powick Bridge I had Maurice *and* the dog. Maurice is now gone to his own command. Boye is tied in the baggage cart."

The Prince put a piece of mutton to his mouth, but suddenly flung it onto the grass. "What the devil?" he shouted, scrambling to his feet as he went running to his horse.

"It's muskets—our muskets firing from the ditch!" called out an officer.

Mounting, Rupert cried out, "The Roundheads—they attack us! To horse! To horse!"

In the cart, huddled under coverlets against the approach of the rain, Hugh Joliffe heard the sound of the muskets. He sat up slowly, flung the covers off, and listened. He knew what it meant. The battle had begun. From under

his coat the page took the small sharp knife he always carried with him. He caught Boye, who had not expected such a
sudden movement, by the collar and with one swift jerk cut
the rope.

"Go, Boye! Go, find Rupert!" he cried to the dog. As
the startled poodle leaped out of the back of the cart to the
ground, Hugh stood up and laughed, his knife still in his
hand. He did not see the old man in the cart drawn up next
to his stand up, too, to peer at him. He did not know that in
a flash of summer lightning the carter had marked out the
glitter of the knife blade in his hand as well as the dog's
jumping free out of the cart. But then Hugh heard the old
man's croaking shout, "I saw ye, lad. I saw ye cut the
Prince's dog free!"

Boye ran, ran toward the sounds he heard. He did not
heed the men about him who, having received Rupert's second order of the day, hastened to their horses. Boye knew
the direction he sought. He ran toward the gunfire.

Within a few minutes he came to the ditch, the ditch
Cromwell's men streamed across. For a long moment the
dog stood, uncertain. Then a Cavalier in the ditch called to
him by name. The poodle bounded toward him, but almost
at once changed his course. As he ran along, some Roundhead cavalrymen at a gallop came slashing through the
stagnant water directly toward him. Under the lightning-
struck sky he marked their grim faces as they bent low for

cover. He heard their awful shouts. Under the sky he saw their horses' open mouths, straining at their bits.

Boye turned about and darted toward the Cavalier lines. As the white poodle ran, Elnathan Parmenter marked him. "The witch cur," he yelled.

In the terrible noise of battle few heard Parmenter, who galloped toward Boye, a fast-moving white blur on the field. Parmenter saw the course the dog made—toward Rupert, who swept forward from the right to throw his force against Cromwell's cavalry. At a diagonal Parmenter gained on Boye with his pistol primed and ready.

The dog's speed was no match for that of Parmenter's horse. As the Roundhead passed behind the poodle, he took careful aim and fired downward. His bullet caught Boye through the spine, and he fell into the tall grass of the moor.

Rupert did not know that Boye lay dying upon the battlefield. He had scarcely got onto his mount before the Roundheads were upon him. His men had been driven back. The Prince had rallied them; then the Roundheads had pushed him back once more. Finally the enemy and the Cavaliers had come to sword point; there they stayed, trading blow for blow.

Before long the Prince heard the ringing shouts from the right of his line. From them he knew that battle had commenced along its entire length. The Cavaliers had grave troubles. They were being little by little, foot by foot, driven off the field. Cromwell's well-disciplined soldiers were winning the stormy night. Hundreds of Roundheads poured over the ditch. Cavalier regiments outnumbered, broke and ran.

Rupert's own men had faltered and broken. When he came to rally them, it was of no use. He called to them, "Follow me." They tried to obey but were thrust up against Cromwell's solid bank of troopers. Cromwell's line could not be shattered—not by the Prince or by any other man.

The Prince's bold troopers, the victors of so many fierce charges, fled before the Roundheads. Elsewhere on the field, other Cavaliers broke. Within minutes the defeat of the King's forces was accomplished.

Rupert almost at once found himself entirely alone. Knowing he had lost the day, he leaped his mount over a fence to safety in a bean field.

Hugh Joliffe had not waited—once his treachery had been discovered by the carter. A horse was tethered to the back of the baggage wagon, a spare horse in case one of the cart horses fell lame. The page ran to it, untied it, and scrambled onto its back.

He would escape to safety far away from the battle and from the old man who had seen him. Now he must save himself and forget his master and the Austrian dog.

Hugh was not an expert rider and had no saddle. His horse was wild with excitement, for all that it was only a poor nag. It wore but a hackamore, and without a bit Hugh could not control it. The old cart horse galloped headlong in the direction of the battle in spite of Hugh's wild cries of "Stop." The horse took him into the thick of jostling, slashing Cavaliers and Roundheads.

A young Roundhead cornet who had just shot a Cavalier with his pistol had paused for breath beside a hedgerow at the edge of the battle when he saw the tall boy coming toward him on the old horse. Without a second thought he spurred his mount forward. With one chop of his sword the Roundhead killed Hugh Joliffe, who had ridden into the melee wearing the fatal broad green sash of the Cavaliers.

In the morning the victorious Oliver Cromwell rode over the field of Marston Moor as Rupert had ridden over the field at Powick Bridge. His aide and other officers rode near him, rejoicing that the tide of war had now definitely turned in their favor. When they came to a group of Roundhead bodies, one of them dismounted. A trooper lay facedown in the grass, his sword arm outstretched, his sword fallen from his fingers.

"Turn him over so I may see his face," Cromwell ordered.

Obediently, with the toe of his boot, the officer turned over the corpse of Elnathan Parmenter. His coat was dark with blood. He'd been shot through the heart, killed by an unknown Cavalier.

"A brave man," said General Cromwell. "His sword

within inches of his hand. He would have used it more. So—he died! See to his burial."

The Roundheads rode on slowly, this time toward the northern edge of the field. Hugh Joliffe lay there, on his side, his arms outstretched exactly as he had fallen. The Roundhead cornet's sword had caught him on the side of his head. Because of his position, the terrible wound and the blood could not be seen.

"A beautiful lad," remarked Cromwell. "The Cavaliers now recruit troopers from the cradle and send them out weaponless in their green scarves. London apprentices I will accept in my army, but not innocent babes. See to it this child is given decent burial in a churchyard."

"Aye," replied one of his officers, who looked up expectantly as a trooper came at a canter across the field toward them.

"What is it?" asked Cromwell's aide.

" 'Tis the dog—the witch cur!" the trooper exclaimed excitedly.

Cromwell nodded. "What of him? I recall the witch dog well. Essex's troopers kept him caged until someone set him free."

"He lies dead, too, here!" said the excited man.

"I will see the dog again!" Cromwell told him.

Walking his horse slowly, he came to stand over the body of Boye. The poodle lay alone, for no sprawled corpse was within ten feet of him in any direction.

"It is Rupert's luck. I saw the beast in London!" said the Roundhead victor.

"What shall we do with him?" asked an officer.

Cromwell turned his heavy face to the man. "Bury him here. Bury him, of course! I do not make war on animals. I may again face Rupert, but I made no war on his dog— witch cur though superstitious fools called him. Whatever the animal may have been, he was a soldier's dog. Like a soldier he lived; like a soldier he died. That honor I will do him!"

The old carter was taken prisoner by the Roundheads and for three days not let go. Then he drove off alone to York. He had heard Roundhead gossip of the death of the witch cur and talk of the peculiar death of the green-sashed lad who rode "weaponless" into the battle of Marston Moor. A wise old man, he guessed it was Hugh—and he knew the dog was Boye and how he had come to die there.

In York the wagon driver kept to himself. Rumor there soon informed him that Rupert had learned of the death of his dog from a Yorkshire farmer, and that the Prince was concerned about the strange disappearance of his page.

"I will not tell him—not of the cut rope," said the carter to himself. The next day he deserted to Liverpool, his home, knowing that Prince Rupert would not go that way again soon.

* * *

At the head of six thousand troopers the Prince left York a few days after the battle. He rode with them past the field of Marston Moor, then turned south, heading for Wales once more. As he passed the now sunlit field Rupert reined in his horse, his troopers halting behind him.

He looked to the north and said aloud, but so softly no man heard him, "Boye! Hugh! I will not forget!"

Authors' Note

THE PEOPLE IN THIS BOOK

Most of the people who appear here as characters were actual historical figures; some, however, are fictional. Chief among the latter is our Hugh Joliffe. We know for a fact that Prince Rupert was sent a page at Linz, but we do not know his name or what he looked like. We have made him Hugh. Other significant characters who are fictional are Elnathan Parmenter, Captain Addison, and Arbela Mary Claycomb.

The lives of the historical persons who appear as characters in this book are fascinating. Here are some background details about them.

THE QUEEN OF BOHEMIA AND HER FAMILY

PRINCE RUPERT. Prince Rupert was born in 1619, the third son of Elizabeth, Queen of Bohemia, and Frederick V, King of Bohemia. When he was only six weeks old his family was driven out of Bohemia and took refuge in Holland.

At the age of fourteen Rupert began his career as a soldier. In 1636 he came to England and met King Charles I, who liked him, and who later appointed him to lead his cavalry in the Civil War.

We have described the battles in which Rupert took part as accurately and as simply as possible. After the Prince's disastrous defeat at Marston Moor, he did not quit soldiering. He relieved the sieges of several towns and fought at the Battle of Naseby. But in 1646 Oxford was surrendered to the Roundheads, and Rupert and his brother, Maurice, were ordered out of England by Parliament.

Rupert went to France and there entered the service of the French King as an officer in his army. In 1648 he went with the exiled Prince Charles of England to Holland and with him sailed out to fight a Roundhead admiral at sea. The next year, the year Charles I was executed, found Rupert in Ireland, trying to capture Roundhead ships which he hoped to sell to raise money for the Prince's armies. Many folk called him a "pirate" for his naval activities.

Charles II was very fond of his cousin, and in many ways they were alike, though Charles, who was very lively, often thought Rupert too somber.

Rupert spent six years in Germany, going there in 1654 while Oliver Cromwell ruled England. When Charles was invited home to his throne in 1660, Rupert came back, too. Charles II made him a member of his Privy Council and gave him various high commands in the royal navy. During the latter part of his life most of Rupert's fighting was confined to the sea.

After Boye's death the Prince did not keep a dog for many years. When he finally got one, it was not white—but black. After the Marston Moor death of his poodle, men noticed Rupert became even more melancholy and harsh. He never married. Throughout his life he seems to have truly loved but four beings—Maurice, Sophie, Will Legge, and his dog, Boye. The Roundheads criticized Rupert's attachment to Boye in a pamphlet of 1644. It said about Marston Moor, "Here also was slain that accursed cur which is here mentioned by the way because the Prince's dog hath been much spoken of, and was prized by his master more than creatures of much more worth."

Rupert was famed in the seventeenth century for more than military exploits. He was a good artist and liked science. He de-

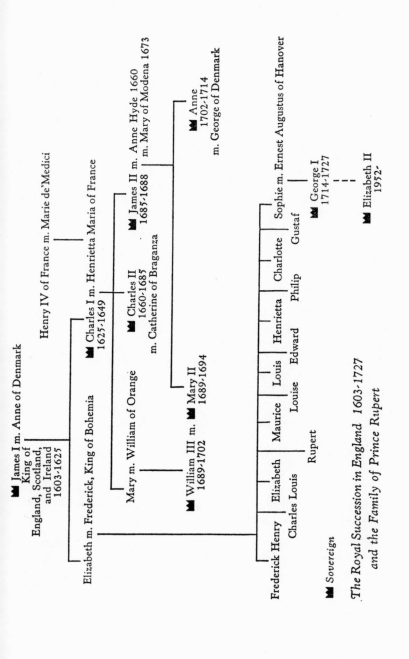

*The Royal Succession in England 1603-1727
and the Family of Prince Rupert*

vised improvements in gunpowder, cannon, and small firearms; and he experimented with metals and glass.

In 1682 Rupert died. He lies buried in Westminster Abbey. At the time of his death his titles were Count Palatine of the Rhine, Duke of Bavaria, Duke of Cumberland, and Earl of Holderness.

PRINCE MAURICE. Maurice was the fourth son of Frederick V, King of Bohemia and Elizabeth, his Queen. He was born in 1620 and, like his brother, Rupert, spent his entire childhood in exile in Holland. Like Rupert, Maurice went to war at a very early age.

At the beginning of the English Civil War Maurice was often with his brother but later went to serve under other Cavalier officers. Yet the fortunes of war often brought them together again. He was not at Marston Moor, but was with Rupert at Naseby a year later where the Cavaliers were also defeated.

Maurice, too, left England in 1646. He served in the army of the Stadtholder of the Netherlands and in 1648 rejoined Rupert in his piratical career off the coast of Ireland. Rupert early in 1649 went to the West Indies, and Maurice went with him. The trip was a long one with many stops along the way: Portugal, France, Africa, and the Cape Verde Islands. In 1652 the two Princes reached the West Indies, but in September of that year Maurice's ships were caught by a storm. Three out of the four foundered. Maurice was drowned at sea.

Historians do not consider Maurice the soldier that his brother was. He was bold and brave but no strategist. He did not command well nor did he share Rupert's wondrous luck, for while Rupert went through the Civil War unscathed by sword or bullet, Maurice was often wounded.

THE QUEEN OF BOHEMIA. Elizabeth Stuart was born in 1596, the daughter of King James I of England and his Queen, Anne of Denmark. She was married in 1613 to a German prince, Frederick. With him she went to Germany to live. In 1619 he was offered the crown of Bohemia, a crown that the Austrians thought should belong by rights to their prince. Frederick accepted the crown, but with his wife was soon driven out of Bohemia by Austrian armies. As a matter of fact, his reign was so brief, only lasting for some months, that he was nicknamed the Winter's King. The war between his Protestant adherents and the supporters of his Roman Catholic enemies developed eventually into the ghastly conflict known as the Thirty Years War. At first Elizabeth and Frederick went to Germany; then, unwelcome there, traveled to Holland where they were favored by the Stadtholder. By this time Elizabeth had several children, Rupert and two older sons and a daughter. More were to come—among them Maurice, Sophie, and other daughters and sons. In 1632 her husband died and the exiled queen lived on with her children and her menagerie of dogs and monkeys at The Hague.

Elizabeth was a woman who enjoyed excellent health and who liked riding, hunting, and lively entertainments of all sorts. She was charming, witty, wildly extravagant, and constantly in debt. Her misfortunes and the early deaths of several of her children did not over-dismay her.

In 1661 after Charles II had become King, Elizabeth came, too, to England. She saw Rupert often there; mother and son seemed affectionate toward one another. By this time he was her oldest surviving son; to him she left her jewels when she died in 1662.

SOPHIE. Sophie, who was born in 1630, was the next to the last of the many children of the Queen of Bohemia. She was certainly one of the sprightliest of the lot and has left interesting memoirs of what it was like to live in her exiled mother's court. Too, she is the source of many of the anecdotes about Rupert and Maurice. Sophie's life was spent on the continent—chiefly in Germany. In 1658 she married a German prince, Ernest Augustus of Hanover; in 1660 a son was born to them, George Lewis. This son was in 1714 invited to come to England to be King. He is known as George I and is the ancestor of the present Queen of England.

Because of this son, Sophie, who died in 1714, in a sense is the most important of the children of the Queen of Bohemia—although England certainly affected her life little except through her brothers.

THE ROYAL FAMILY OF ENGLAND

KING CHARLES I. A younger brother of Elizabeth, Queen of Bohemia, Charles was born in 1600. In 1625 he became King of England. That same year he wed Henrietta Maria, the daughter of a French king and the sister of the King of France.

Like his father, James I, Charles I did not work well with the English Parliament. For years King and Parliament quarreled over all sorts of issues—the King's favorite courtiers, money, religion, taxes, and other matters.

On January 10, 1642 the King rode out of London. He would not return again for seven years, and then only to die.

For seven years off and on, his armies of Cavaliers fought the armies of Parliament, sometimes winning, sometimes losing. In 1648 Charles, thinking that the Scots would send troops to support him, signed a secret treaty with them. The Scottish army was defeated by Cromwell and other Roundheads. The King was left alone.

The Roundhead army and certain members of the Parliament decided that Charles was the cause of all England's troubles and determined to rid themselves of him for all time. They had him brought to London. There he went on trial for his life on a charge of treason against England. He was found "guilty." On January 30th, 1649 Charles I was beheaded—the first and only English King ever to be executed.

QUEEN HENRIETTA MARIA. In 1609 Henrietta Maria was born to the Queen of France, Marie de' Medici. The little girl really never knew her royal father, Henry IV, for he was assassinated a few months after her birth.

In 1625 she was married to Charles I. At first the little French princess detested her English husband but before long grew to love him.

For the most part the English people did not like their French-born Queen. Her religion was Roman Catholic; theirs was Protestant. They did not understand her or trust her, and they did not like her influence over the King. Moreover, they disliked her extravagance and her giddiness.

Henrietta Maria was a brave woman. She labored on the continent gathering arms, ammunition, and soldiers for the Cavaliers during the Civil War and she often shared the dangers of the war with the King. More than once she was fired upon by Roundhead soldiers as she traveled about England. The King feared for her safety and in the summer of 1644 she was sent away to France. She did not see her husband again.

For five years—until Charles's death in 1649—the Queen worked trying to get assistance from France. Here she continued to live until 1660 when her oldest son, Charles II, came to the throne of England. Then she, like so many others, returned to his court.

Henrietta Maria did not like England's climate, however. In 1665 she went home to France and in 1669 there died.

KING CHARLES II. Charles II was born in 1630 to Charles I and Henrietta Maria. Far more intelligent, quick-witted, and far-sighted than his father, Charles was well educated by private tutors.

With his father and younger brother, James, Charles traveled about England during the Civil War. He was present at Edgehill; by the time he was fifteen years old he had received an important military command. In March of 1645 the Prince left his father forever and rode away to the west of England. A year later when the war had gone badly for the Cavaliers, the young Prince took ship for safety in the Scilly Isles. Later he went to France to join his mother. When he learned that his father was to be executed by Parliament, the youth did all he could to save him, even sending

Parliament a blank piece of paper with his signature, telling them to "fill in" the terms they chose to save the King.

In 1650 Charles, who was now King, came to Scotland and was there crowned. He fought in a Scots-English army against Cromwell twice, but both times lost. In 1651 he escaped by the hair of his head once more to exile in France.

The next ten years were sad ones for the throneless King. While Cromwell ruled, Charles stayed in Holland, France, and Germany. He was so poor that his clothing was threadbare; he could not afford to keep a coach. He often quarreled with his mother and was in general a very unhappy man.

All this came to an end after Cromwell's death, Charles was then invited back to England. He came in May 1660, and took his throne.

Charles was not yet married—although the Queen of Bohemia had attempted to marry him to her Sophie, his cousin, Rupert's sister. In 1661 he married at last—a Portuguese princess. They had no children.,

When he died in 1685, his throne went to his younger brother, James.

Modern historians think that Charles II was one of England's better kings. He was humane, easygoing, remarkably intelligent, and not at all impressed with himself and his own dignity. He got along with Parliament where his father could not. His brother, James, was also to lose the throne, but clever Charles II kept it for twenty-five years.

KING JAMES II. The second son of Charles I and Henrietta Maria, James II, was born in 1633.

Like his older brother, Charles II, James for a time traveled about England with his father during the Civil War. One of the conditions of the surrender of Oxford—the same conditions which sent Rupert and Maurice into exile—was that James be put in the custody of Parliament. He, a younger brother and a sister were confined by a Roundhead nobleman but were permitted to see their prisoner-father now and then. In 1648 dressed in women's clothing James escaped to Europe where he lived at The Hague for a time.

From 1649 to 1660 James also knew poverty and unhappiness. In 1652 he joined the army of the King of France and rose to the rank of lieutenant general.

James came to London with Charles in 1660 as Lord High Admiral of England. Later that year he married an Englishwoman. By her he had two daughters.

While his brother ruled, James devoted himself to affairs of the navy. James displeased the people of England by his interest in the Roman Catholic religion. They were very angry when he became a convert to it.

James's English wife died. In 1673 he wed Mary of Modena, an Italian princess and a Roman Catholic. In 1685 he succeeded to his childless brother's throne. For three years he ruled England as a thoroughly unpopular monarch.

The English people were terrified of having a Roman Catholic line of kings. They were willing to tolerate James II as long as he had no Roman Catholic children, but when his wife presented him in 1688 with a son, the people rose up against James and drove him out of the country.

He took refuge with his wife and child in France, never to return to England though he tried again and again, and his descendants tried through much of the next century to regain his throne.

James's daughters by his English wife were Protestant. The oldest of them, Mary, married to a Dutch prince, was invited to become Queen and her husband King. William III and Mary II reigned together until his death in 1702. Because they had no children, the youngest daughter of James II, Anne, now succeeded as Queen. She died in 1714 without any surviving children. It was then that the son of Sophie, Prince Rupert's sister, became the King of England—King George I.

OTHER HISTORICAL PERSONS

THE EARL OF ARUNDEL. Thomas Howard was the second Earl of Arundel. He was born in 1586. Arundel was a plain, quiet man but a great lover of art, as well as an extremely well educated person. In 1621 he was made earl-marshal of England and in 1630 was sent to the Queen of Bohemia to bring her back to England, but she would not come. At this time Arundel developed a fondness for her rowdy family, which would account for his sending the poodle to Rupert, the prisoner of the emperor of Austria.

The art world owes a great debt to Arundel. He brought the works of Leonardo da Vinci, Raphael, Holbein, Coreggio, and others to England. The "Arundel marbles," a group of statuary, are particularly famous.

The earl eventually settled with his grandsons in Italy, where he died in 1646.

THE EARL OF ESSEX. Robert Devereux, the third Earl of Essex, was born in 1591. He was a quiet man who would have appreciated a quiet life—one he never had. When the King's troubles arose with Parliament, Essex chose its side. In 1642 he was named General of the Parliamentary army—chiefly because of his interest in the Roundhead cause, not because of his military prowess.

Personally brave, Essex was not a good general. He made many blunders and quarreled with other Roundhead commanders. He was soon overshadowed by Cromwell. In April of 1645 Essex resigned as general; he died the next year.

OLIVER CROMWELL. Of all of England's great men Oliver Cromwell stands forth as one of the greatest. He was born in 1599. Until 1642 he seems to have led the simple life of a country gentleman—except that he was elected to Parliament in 1628.

Cromwell learned all that he knew of tactics and strategy from books. He had excellent good sense, a dislike of King Charles's high-handed policies, and a great interest in the rise to power of Parliament.

When the Roundhead armies formed under the Earl of Essex, Cromwell joined them as a captain of cavalry. He was at Edgehill. It was there he decided that the army he soldiered in needed "spirit." He resolved to mould his own force, a force of good, religious men. And so he did—the famous New Model Army, one of the armies renowned in history for its discipline and "spirit." At Marston Moor this army met Rupert's and defeated it. At Marston Moor Prince Rupert, himself, gave Cromwell's men their nick-name, the Ironsides.

Cromwell fought again and again throughout the late 1640's and the early 1650's. Few Cavalier forces could stand against him. After the death of the King no man in England was half so power-ful as he, and in 1653 Parliament named him Lord Protector of the Realm.

His rule, which lasted until his death in 1658, was a stern one. His son tried to govern England as his successor, but lacked the force of his father and resigned. In 1660 Parliament, seeking a ruler, issued an invitation for Charles II to come home to his throne.

SOURCES

For this novel we have chiefly used *The Great Civil War 1642-1646* by Lt. Col. Alfred H. Burne and Lt. Col. Peter Young, 1959; *Prince Rupert the Cavalier* by Clennell Wilkinson, 1934; and *Ru-pert, Prince Palatine* by Eva Scott, 1900. Wilkinson's book con-tains several portraits of Rupert. It also has two cartoons of Boye from Roundhead pamphlets of the period.

Another source was the *Dictionary of National Biography*. We have also consulted Eliot Warburton's three-volume work, *Memoirs of Prince Rupert and the Cavaliers, Including Their Pri-vate Correspondence,* and the Earl of Clarendon's classic, *History of the Rebellion,* as well as manuscript material.

In checking the conversational speech of the characters in this novel we have used C. T. Onions' *Shorter Oxford English Dictionary Based on Historical Principles.* We have attempted to give the flavor of everyday talk with some accuracy. Too, we have made every effort to depict the actual settings and state the exact weather conditions, for instance, the unusually cold autumn and winter that occurred during the first years of the Civil War. We have named the principals involved on both sides in those Civil War battles in which Boye and his master took part.

John and Patricia Beatty
London, England
February 1967

About the Authors

Both John and Patricia Beatty were born in Portland, Oregon, and went to Reed College there. After graduation, Mrs. Beatty studied at the University of Washington, in Seattle, and Dr. Beatty received his M.A. from Stanford University and his Ph.D. from the University of Washington. He is now a professor at the University of California, his subject being English history of the seventeenth and eighteenth centuries.

The Beattys were married in 1950, and later lived in Wilmington, Delaware, and London, England. Dr. Beatty served in the United States Army in World War II, in the European Theater. Mrs. Beatty has taught high-school English and history. She also held a position as a science and technical librarian, and then worked as a member of the technical information staff of the explosives department of the DuPont Company. She lived for some years in Coeur d'Alene, Idaho, and has had several novels published by Morrow about the American West.

While they were writing *Witch Dog,* the Beattys spent one winter in England where they lived within a mile of the towns of Brentford and Turnham Green, which were scenes of the Civil War action described in the book. The Beattys now live in Riverside, California, with their daughter, Ann Alexandra, born in 1957.